AFTER
THE DUST
SETTLES

CALIFORNIA DREAMING BOOK III

STACEY JOHNSTON

STRATTON
—PRESS—
Publishing Life

AFTER THE DUST SETTLES
Copyright © 2019 **Stacy Johnston**

Stratton Press Publishing
831 N Tatnall Street Suite M #188,
Wilmington, DE 19801
www.stratton-press.com
1-888-323-7009

ISBN (Paperback): 978-1-64345-557-0
ISBN (Ebook): 978-1-64345-773-4

Printed in the United States of America

AUTHOR BIO

Stacey Johnston resides in one of the southern suburbs of Perth, Western Australia, with her husband, four children and a lovable Alaskan malamute called Storm.

At one time or another, each of us has wished that our lives reflected those of the characters we read in books or watched on our television screens. As a child, Stacey was no different and found she could create stories in her head, stories where her characters could come alive and she could escape when life around her became difficult.

Leaving home at seventeen, she moved from family member to family member, trying to find her place. During those early years, alcohol became her closest friend, and her characters and stories in her head really started to blossom. It was not until she met the man who would become the father to her oldest two children that she started to settle down.

For the next twelve years, Stacey dedicated her life to her partner and their two beautiful children. Her stories were continuing to grow, but so was her desire to put them on paper and share them. Tragically, after losing her partner to a heart attack, her grip on reality started to slide, and it was during this time that her characters evolved.

During her time of need, Stacey found a soul mate who would later become her husband and give her two more equally beautiful children. With his love, support, and encouragement Stacey finally found the courage to put her characters and stories onto paper.

Stacey's hope is that other readers love her characters as much as she does. Her wish is that they are caught up in their stories, experiencing their joy and pain just as she has over the years.

ITALIAN GLOSSARY

Grandma – nonna
Daughter – figlia
Son – figlio
Grandpa – nonno
Mother – madre
Father – padre
Brother – fratello
Sister – sorella
My angel – mio angelo

CHAPTER ONE

Sometimes, following your heart means losing your mind.

PRESENT

Sean

"Sean, darling, please take a break," my mother pleads from the doorway. "You have been hiding in here all day."

There's a sadness to her voice that's been there since the day we lost Sherlyn. It's small and soft and full of despair each time she addresses me.

"Please join us," she quietly requests. "I have your supper ready."

My stomach reacts at the mere mention of food, grumbling loudly. My eyes are starting to get heavy, and my brain hasn't been functioning properly for the last hour, so maybe it wouldn't hurt to have a break.

I can bear to see the sadness I hear in her voice reflecting in her eyes, so keeping my attention on the screen before me, I attempt to appease her. "Yes, just let me log off."

For the last ten months, since Sherlyn's death, Hawke and I have been working on bringing down the Alexandria family. Although they weren't responsible for the mind-set of the sick son of a bitch who murdered her, they are the reason she had a target on her head to begin with. Someone needs to be held accountable for what Vincent Salvatore did, and that someone is going to be Jason Alexandria.

There is more than enough evidence against Jason to bring his organization down, but we still can't secure the monetary link between him and Vincent. Hawke wants to wait so he can make sure that this time, Jason goes away for good.

Unfortunately, everything I have found to date is above-board and legal, or so it would seem anyway. Whoever handles the money side of their organization is really fucking good at hiding shit, but I will crack it eventually. What I need to do is work out how these direct deposits and the account they end up in are linked. I have been researching offshore banking during what little spare time I allow myself. If there is a link, I will find it. You can count on it.

All we do know, for now, is that the money they transfer bounces a few times before it reaches its final destination. Why it does this, we still don't know, but what we are sure of is the name on the account is a fake one. There is no known person by that name. To make things even more intriguing, the date of birth used was Sherlyn's.

My mother is probably right, though. What I really need tonight is time away from these monitors. Maybe I just need another assignment to escape the ghost that haunts my dreams. I'd take anything to help silence my troubling thoughts.

The most likely outcome will see me visiting my sister back in Solana Beach. She has been pestering my father for months to get me to go, but I keep resisting.

I love Sophie, don't get me wrong, but it's not her I'm struggling to face—*it's Stephen*. I feel as though I don't belong there anymore now that Ben, Kyle, Luke, and Stephen have moved into our home. It was around that time when I alienated myself and became a stranger to those closest to me.

It couldn't hurt to head back, even if it's just for a short while. I do miss Soph and her stupidity so much. Hell, I miss everyone, but that dark cloud that shadows the group now is just something I haven't wanted to face. I still feel at fault somehow for Sherlyn's death. *I always will.*

After another quiet meal, I make my way back to my room. When my father moved my mother and I to our current location, I chose the bedroom located at the rear of Hawke's home. It was my way of avoiding prying eyes.

It's been no secret I preferred my seclusion. I've stayed hidden away in my sanctuary to avoid the sad glances and worried words of my mother, who now knows how I feel about Sherlyn. She's a very intuitive person, so I've no doubt she's probably known since the beginning. If I'm honest, it was stupid of me to think that she wouldn't notice.

The one thing that has saddened me over these past few months is watching my mother struggle to come to terms with the senseless murder of someone she'd grown close to. Sherlyn became an adoptive daughter to my parents, so much more than the foster child label child protective services gave her. Both my parents took her death hard, especially my mother.

She may give a brave appearance, but deep down, she is a fragile, gentle woman at the best of times—a beautiful woman with her own demons, ones you will never hear her speak about, ones that involve her own parents. What devastated her the most was knowing how hard they fought to give Sherlyn a normal life, only for it to be taken away so suddenly. Her struggle led to her spending a few weeks with her brothers, my uncle Callum to be exact, at his Californian home.

My guilt, though, goes way beyond that of my mother's. The guilt that I harbor is for my selfishness and the way I treated her. For those short few weeks, I chose to place a wedge between us, staying away because it hurt too much being in her presence. I'll be direct, it was for no other reason than I couldn't bear to see her and Stephen together. It just confirmed that she would never be mine.

What it amounted to was a whole lot of nothing. I wasted the precious time I had left with her by avoiding her. In the end, she was taken away from us all, and that is something none of us can ever get back.

Hawke confided in me after she was gone that the things he saw that day echo throughout his thoughts often, and that's exactly how I feel right now. There is a black-and-white version of the day Sherlyn died playing on a loop, constantly in my thoughts, and it's depressing as all fuck. I just want it to stop.

I became numb when the doctor told us that Sherlyn hadn't made it. I didn't believe him at first. All I could think was, *No, they must have the wrong girl*, because the one we brought in was still alive and breathing.

Surely, what he was telling us couldn't be true. *It wasn't allowed to be.*

When the news started sinking in, my whole body caved, slumping against the wall. In the distance, I could hear my sister wailing, although at that time, she sounded a lot farther away than the mere feet it was. At first, I tried to console both her and my mother, but their blubbering was only forcing me to sink faster. I ended up having to shut them out, focusing on anything but the reason we were all gathered.

As soon as my parents left with Stephen to view her body, I ran, leaving the hospital on foot. I spent endless hours just walking. I couldn't tell you how many blocks I walked. All I know is, I eventually ended up on Atlantic Avenue, heading toward the water. I was lost, a withdrawn nobody in a sea of endless faces. I spoke to no one and kept my gaze on the concrete path beneath me.

I could feel my cell buzzing in my pocket, but I paid no attention to it. When I finally did check it, I found that Sophie and my mother had tried endlessly to reach me. There were well over forty missed calls between them. I don't know what stopped them in the end, but I was grateful. All I needed at that time was to be by myself. My head needed clearing in a way that neither of them could assist me with.

That was the day I found another way of escaping the demons in my head for a while.

TEN MONTHS EARLIER

"Hey, sugar, why the sad face?" a sexy voice drawls from behind me.

The sound of her voice startles me. I don't know how long I have been sitting on this bank, but my feet are fucking aching now.

Where the hell am I?

Looking around, I notice a cute little brunette leaning against the light pole, gazing at me dreamily. Surely, she can't be staring at me. If she is I don't understand why the fuck she would be.

"Whatever you are selling, I'm not interested," I holler over my shoulder in a show of disinterest. Returning my attention to the water, I try to ignore her.

"Oh, I'm not selling anything, honey, just making an observation," her now sultry voice replies, causing my cock to betray me.

Fuck me.

Moving slightly, I try not to make it too obvious to the vixen behind me that I'm rearranging myself.

"Then leave, because I'm not in a talkative mood, and I don't want to be fucking rude."

A comment like that would have had my sister storming off. Thinking she had left, I continue staring out into the abyss, my vision not really focusing on anything in particular. As tears well in my eyes, thoughts of Sherlyn take over, flooding my head with memories of her from the night before.

Oh my god, she looked stunning at that restaurant. Her beautiful face looked relaxed, like she didn't have a care in the world. Little did she, or any of us, realize, just twenty-four hours later, the butcher who had cornered her would, in fact, succeed in murdering her. I honestly doubt any of us actually believed he would get to her, but fuck, were we all wrong.

Movement beside me scares the crap out of me, making me jump. "What the fuck," I yell, squirming backward.

A snigger beside me alerts me that instead of leaving, my new brunette friend has chosen to stick around.

"Relax, sugar, I'm not going to hurt you." She laughs, sitting her ass down on the grass beside me.

As I cautiously stare at her, she inches closer, giving me the opportunity to get a better look at her.

Whoa, what can I say?

I can't believe how fucking gorgeous this girl is. I wonder if she's a model.

With looks like my mystery girl, I can't imagine her being anything else.

It's embarrassing, the hold she has on me right now, but I can't seem to stop staring at her. Her flawless face, or more precisely, her emerald-green eyes, are having a mesmerizing effect on me. They are bright and gorgeous, capable of dragging you under. If she were a river, I'd be drowning right now.

I'm trying to break the hold she has on me, but fuck me, it's not that easy.

A smile comes to my face as I watch her struggle to reign in her long wavy hair in the wind. My eyes drop to her mouth, watching as she slips her tongue across her bottom lip to moisten it. My own mouth becomes dry as fuck as I take in the sight before me.

If it wasn't before, my cock is now standing to attention, straining behind my boxers, screaming to be set freed.

Her lips curl at the side, obviously noticing my shameless gawking. "See something you like, darling?" she drawls at me once more.

Looking further down, I finally get a good look at the rest of her body, and yep, my cock is in love. Her fucking tits barely fit the tank she is attempting to squeeze them into, and those legs of hers go on for miles. It's not helping that the shorts she's wearing leave absolutely nothing to the imagination.

In short, this girl is hot as fuck.

"There isn't anything about you that I don't like, babe, but now's not the time," I finally confess.

I'm shocked at how much confidence I'm showing right now. Since when do I have the balls for this shit?

Oh yeah, since last night. I smirk to myself.

"I could relieve some of that stress for twenty bucks," I hear her say.

She's unrelenting, and the sass in her voice amuses me. I don't know if I am in shock, or disbelief over her abruptness.

"Wait…what?"

I'm now staring at her again.

"Did you just say you'd blow me for twenty bucks?"

Okay, now it's definitely disbelief I'm feeling.

Continuing, I taunt, "Why would I pay you, when some random was on her knees blowing me last night in a men's room for nothing."

Her response is instant.

"What makes you think I can't do it better?"

Touché, I'll give her that, but I'm still not paying her twenty bucks to suck my cock.

"Planning on doing it on this bank, are you?" I snarl.

I don't mean to be nasty, but she is grating on my nerves now. What part of no doesn't she get?

"I've done far worse on this bank," she quickly throws back at me.

Taking another look in her direction, she has a sad, void look, but for all I know, it's just an act to mug me. Sighing, I give it a few minutes before responding to her.

"Sorry, babe, timing is bad. I'm far from in the mood, regardless of how hot you are."

Rising, I turn away from her once more. There are two women who are going to remove my testicles if I don't let them know I'm okay. I should probably call at least one of them. It's not like I can sit here all night, especially with this ice-cold wind.

"You don't trust me, do you?" she quickly calls.

Stopping, I spin around and stare.

"Why are you persisting?" I know it's wrong, but I can't stop staring at her. "What kind of game are you playing at?"

I'm fucking stunned that she is still trying to work me. What the hell is her deal, anyway?

"I don't play games. I'm just asking a question."

Now she has me curious.

"No, I don't trust you. Are you happy now? For all I know, some big ugly dude is hiding behind that tree waiting to attack me."

The laugh that escapes her throat is something I would expect from Ben or Luke, definitely not from a girl. I'm glad she finds me so fucking amusing, but right now I don't have the patience for her bullshit. In a different time and place, that deep, loud laughter of hers would amuse me.

"What's so funny?" I growl.

"You." She giggles.

Scratching the back of my head, I just gawk at her. One thing is for sure, she's not like any girl I've ever met before. I don't know what I'm supposed to make of this one. She really does have me at a loss.

"I won't hurt you, sugar, and I swear, there's no dude hiding behind a tree." Standing, she shakes the grass off her ass, moving toward me, stopping only when we are inches apart. "It's just me and you, and my offer to relieve whatever the hell is wrong with you."

With her breath on my neck, she leans in, using one hand to gently grip my face as she pulls my head closer to her own.

Whispering, she says, "Let me help you. I know something is wrong. I'm not interested in your money. All I want is you."

As if I'm in a trance, I nod and allow her to lead me away from the bank. In this moment, she has me agreeing to whatever she says.

"Don't worry, darling, I'm not dragging you down an alleyway. I live close by."

Releasing my held breath, I sigh. I'm breathing heavier than normal as I give in and let this gorgeous girl lead me to what could possibly be my own death.

How ironic would that be?

Within minutes, we arrive at her apartment, and I have to admit, it's not what I was expecting. Considering the dump that we had to live in a few months ago, I was kind of expecting something similar. She leads me into her living room, and our silence is becoming unsettling. We haven't spoken a word since she grabbed my hand, and I'm yet to work out if this is a good thing.

Staying put, I stand against the wall, right where she leaves me, and watch as she wanders into her kitchen. I look around. The sight before me wasn't anything I'd envisioned at all. My new friend's furnishings are really girlish and definitely not what I was expecting. While I wait for her to return, I take in all the pastel colors she has decorated with and think to myself that maybe my first impression was wrong.

"Sit," she commands, handing me a glass of water.

Bossy little thing, isn't she?

I can't deny being turned on right now.

"What's your story, mystery boy?"

Yep, I was right—she's bossy, all right. I think I like this one.

"What makes you think I have a story?" I offer in return, taking the glass from her.

Gulping it down, I drink every last drop. I hadn't realized just how thirsty I was until I placed that cool water to my lips.

"Thirsty, I see," she replies as I place the glass on her table.

"A girl of a few words," I tease in return.

Not only is her cheekiness amusing me, but she's also making me feel something I shouldn't. There's a reaction she's igniting throughout my body that shouldn't be happening. It's wrong because I shouldn't want this girl in the way I currently do, especially after what has happened today. There is a game of tug-of-war going on with my emotions right now, which I do not like.

"I'm going at your pace, waiting for you to open up to me," my new brunette acquaintance casually informs me. "I won't rush you. Just take your time."

Curling her legs beneath her at the other end of the sofa, she just watches me, waiting for me to open up to her.

"I lost a friend today, a very close friend." Fighting back the emotion, those few words are all I can muster.

"She was murdered," I eventually add.

The realization of what has happened feels like it's finally taking its toll. As much as I'm fighting it, there are tears pooling in my eyes, with my vision becoming blurrier by the second. I know how pathetic I must look, especially being reduced to tears in front of a complete stranger.

Without warning, arms hug me tightly, and a warm face buries itself into my neck. I don't know what to do, or how I'm even supposed to react. I hope she's not looking for me to do something in return because I can't move.

Pulling away, her hands find their way to my face, and she pulls me toward her. "You have to let it out," she quietly declares. "Holding it in will only destroy you. I promise I won't make fun of you or try and stop you."

I am struggling to understand why, but I'm in awe of this girl. She knows absolutely nothing about me, or even what kind of a person I am, and yet she is accepting me on face value. Without thought, she's consoling me as though we are old friends.

"Why do you care?" I quietly ask, holding her stare. "You don't even know me,"

Those smoky brown eyes of hers suddenly mesmerize me. Even if I wanted to turn away, I doubt I could break the trance she's drawn me into. I can do nothing more in this moment of silence but drown in them.

I wonder if she is aware of the undeniable power she possesses.

Gripping my hands, she pulls them into her lap. As she replies to my question, she loudly releases her breath. "Because there is something about you that makes me feel safe."

Pausing, she catches her breath once more. "It's like I already know you, even though we have only just met."

I don't understand her words, but they make me lose control all the same. "I can't stop myself."

Those four tiny words become my undoing, and in a moment of rashness, my hands grasp her face, pulling her closer until our lips are barely touching. Her breath is heavy on my lips, but it only matches my own.

Closing my eyes, I smash my lips to hers, kissing her with a passion I never knew existed in me. I've never kissed anyone like this before, and although I can't explain the need, the more I taste her lips, the hungrier I become. It's as though I can't get enough of her mouth. With my palms gripping her face tighter, I force my tongue through her lips in time to catch the moan she releases. I don't know what it is about this girl or the situation I'm in, but reality seems to slip further away, and I'm losing all control over my actions.

Abruptly, without any warning, this beauty before me suddenly pulls away. In total surrender, I just watch as she flops backward on the sofa, struggling to find her breath. I can definitely relate to how she is feeling because my own body feels as though it's just run a marathon.

How the hell does that happen after just a kiss?

Sitting back up, she creeps closer again, grabbing my hands in hers.

"Please tell me your name." I hear ask, her voice broken, her breathing heavy.

Should I give her my real name, or should I create something else?

"Sean,"

Oh hell.

"Hello, Sean, I'm Hadley."

"That name suits you," I admit, and honestly, it does.

A beautiful name for a beautiful girl.

Well, fuck, listen to me going all pussy.

"I shouldn't want you, but my cock has been hard since I walked through the door. After everything that has happened today, does that make me a bad person?"

Where the hell did that just come from? Will she reject me?

Who the fuck do I think I am?

Now if it were Luke sitting on this sofa, he could get away with saying shit like that. I've no doubt Hadley would have fallen at his feet, but I'm nothing like Luke. I have no idea how to do this stuff.

A chuckle brings me back to earth.

With her hands still in mine, she inches even closer so that her leg is crushed up against my thigh.

"No more wrong than me wanting you to use that hard cock to fuck me right now."

Wait, what? I must be hearing things.

I have to be.

Who says shit like that anyway?

"From the look on your face, you weren't expecting me to say that, were you?" She giggles.

Well, that would be a no, but now my other concern is, should I?

"I won't lie, that's the last thing I expected to come out of your mouth."

She is still smiling at me, and her eyes are nothing like I have ever seen. As she moves herself over me, she places herself in my lap, and it's not hard to miss the amusement behind those beautiful eyes of hers. Resting her arms on my shoulders, her fingers find their way to the hair on the nape of my neck.

Excitement shoots through me, and I swear my cock is the hardest I think it's ever been. I don't think she has any idea how much it's fucking killing me having it confined behind all this material. What isn't helping my cause is the warmth I can feel coming through the flimsy cloth of her shorts. The source of that heat is what I desperately want to explore, but she is torturing me by rubbing herself over my bulge.

I thought inexperience was supposed to make you feel awkward when you're about to lose your virginity, but oddly I haven't felt that way at all. If anything, I just want to maul her and get under her skin like she has mine. She is bringing something primal out in me that I never knew existed. With my arms wrapped around her waist, I pull her in closer to allow me to bury my face between her tits.

I can feel how badly I'm affecting her, because her legs are squeezing my thighs so fucking tightly. The moans flowing from her mouth are driving me crazy, only escalating my need for her, as that pussy of hers rubs along my already throbbing cock.

I know what I want, and that's obviously to be buried as deep as humanly possible in the warmth I can feel.

"Fuck the foreplay, Sean. Get your cock out and fuck me with it already." She moans, pulling my head in even closer.

She is holding on as if her life's depending on it, and if she grips any tighter, she will fucking suffocate me. Without giving me a chance to respond, or do anything for that matter, she jumps up and strips. I wish I could say it was slow and sexy, but this was fast and desperate. Not wanting to disappoint, I quickly follow her direction.

"Tell me you carry condoms," she demands, halting her movements as she waits for my response.

"I don't carry them around, babe. I wasn't planning on getting laid today."

That probably came out harsher than I would have liked, but for fuck's sake, what was she expecting? When she found me, I was wallowing in self-pity after coming from the hospital where Sherlyn had just died. I never anticipated finding myself in a position like this.

Shit! What am I thinking?

I shouldn't be doing this, not now, not so soon.

"Are you questioning yourself?" Hadley murmurs, startling me.

I am, I can't deny that, but my cock seems to have a mind of its own.

Refocusing, I glance up at the body cautiously walking toward me, and just as quickly as they appear, all thoughts of Sherlyn start to drift away. I'm an asshole, and I will surely suffer in hell for wanting this girl in front of me as badly as I do.

"I was, but a part of me wants you too much."

She halts her advance and just watches me momentarily. When I think she is backing out, she picks up her pace and kneels before me.

"I get it, I do," she starts while eagerly looking at my cock. "But this pull between us is too strong to resist. If that makes you a bad person for wanting it, then I am one too, because I can't explain how desperately I want you right now."

Her touch on the tip of my cock as she smooths the condom over me has me bucking off the sofa. If she's not careful, she'll have me fucking exploding before I even get inside of her.

"Not yet," she scolds, placing herself once again over my cock, kneeling above me.

My mouth is drooling as I direct my attention solely on her fucking hot, delectable body. Placing my hands on her hips, I look up to see her watching me...watch her.

"Do it," and that's all the encouragement I need.

My fingers dig into her hips, gripping them tightly as I yank her down onto my cock, pulling her onto me as far as she would go. Hadley's grip on my shoulders tightens, but she doesn't flinch. Her warmth engulfs me, lulling me into a false sense of reality, making me hold her still.

"If that pussy of yours grips my cock any tighter, it's going to cut it off," I spit through gritted teeth.

"You are so fucking tight, Hadley. I fucking love it. Now move!" I demand.

Without missing a beat, Hadley picks up the pace, riding me like she doesn't have a care in the world. I know I have nothing to compare this to, but the way her muscles grip my cock as she slides up and down is fucking amazing.

It's hard to explain the high I'm on. If it makes any sense, it's like I'm here but I'm not. My mind is wandering, erotic fantasies flooding my head. I feel as though I'm watching what's happening from above us, gliding in my own little state of euphoria. The closeness I have with this girl at this exact moment is not like anything I've ever felt before.

I don't know how it's possible, yet she is edging her way deeper under my skin.

My whole body is on fire, and I can feel my balls tightening, creeping back up into my body. It's the strangest sensation that's pulsing throughout my body in the lead-up to my orgasm. I've had plenty of practice when masturbating on my own, but this isn't a sensation I've ever felt before.

"I can't hold this," I call out. "I need to let go," my voice strains as I fight this feeling building inside of me.

"Don't wait for me, babe. I'll be right there with you," Hadley's breathless voice replies, and just like that, my body tenses.

I have to grip her hips to stop her movements as my body starts crashing down from the high it's been on, in preparation for my orgasm to take over. Not once, not twice, but three fucking times my cock convulses inside of her, and I'm in heaven.

I swear, if I died right now, I'd die fucking happy, especially when Hadley's insides gripped me even fucking tighter than they did before her own release.

Finally she slumps over me, allowing her tits to smother my face once more. Although our breathing is labored, my body is relaxed, and my mind is in a state of bliss. Weirdly I don't know what to say. A part of me believes I should wait for her to say something first.

We are still joined, but my cock is starting to soften inside of her, and I really need to urinate. "I'd love nothing more than to stay buried inside you, but I need to move, gorgeous. This bladder of mine needs relieving."

I can feel her laughter before I hear it as she starts cackling, sitting up straighter.

"All right, lover boy, that's normally a chick thing, but I'll move and let you do your business. Just don't be long. I want a repeat performance."

Laughing along with her, I rise off the sofa and pull her into my arms, kissing her roughly. Releasing her, I don't even need to ask, she lifts her arm to point in the direction of her bathroom.

"I'll be waiting in the room next to the bathroom. Don't be long," I hear as I walk away.

Fuck, I need to be back in that warmth of hers. Just the thought is causing me to harden again. Baseball stats, that's what I need right now. That'll help soften me up so that I can at least take my piss.

The door to her room is ajar, and I expected to find her dressed again, but she isn't. She is laying across her bed scrolling through her phone butt naked.

Fuck me, what a sight.

That ass of hers is so fucking tight, but it's her movements that are amusing me. Smiling, I lean against the frame of her door and watch as Hadley swings her legs back and forth, engrossed in whatever she is reading. It's like she's playing a game, moving them so that one leg hits the bed as her other foot taps her ass.

Fucking adorable, that's what it is.

"Are you just going to stand there and stare at my ass, or are you going to come over here and pound it instead?"

Well, that grabbed my attention.

I move my eyes to her face to find she is smirking at me, her eyes mischievously twinkling. Fuck, this girl is something. Her words shot straight to my cock, which is now at full mast again, bobbing against my naked stomach.

"I think that needs my help." She motions toward my cock, her finger curling toward her as if to say, "Come here."

I don't need to be told twice. I make my way to her bed.

Goddamn, it's warm in this bed.

Where the hell am I?

Oh shit! Hadley.

Carefully untangling her from my body, I slip out of the bed. Moving away to find my clothing, I take one final glance back in Hadley's direction. There isn't an inch of her that isn't beautiful, and my memories from last night will stay with me always.

Ah fuck, my clothes are still near her sofa, I realize, hurriedly glancing around the room.

"Slipping out without a goodbye?" she murmurs, adjusting herself so that she is now propped against her pillows.

Leaning with my back against her wall, I sigh loudly. I know I'm an asshole for trying to leave without waking her.

"I'm sorry, Hadley, I need to head back to my family. There will be a search party looking for me since I haven't made contact," I admit dejectedly.

The look she is giving me is one of disbelief, but if she knew my family, she would understand. "I can't even describe the trouble I am in right now."

Fuck, I need to find my phone.

"If you came back to bed, you'd be in trouble. You're making me horny watching you fidgeting against the wall. You do realize you're naked, right?"

What. The. Fuck?

Looking down, I smile as I take in that I am standing against her wall, naked. I'm glad she finds this amusing.

"I'd love nothing more than to crawl back into that bed and spend the day fucking you, but I can't. My father is going to be furious with me for not making contact sooner."

What smile she did have disappears, her gaze at me questioning.

"I'm only seventeen, Hadley. I probably should have mentioned that sooner," I answer, assuming that was what her look was for, considering I mentioned my father.

"I don't care about your age, lover boy. I'm just wondering why your father is troubling you."

She's a godsend, this girl. It's a shame I won't have the opportunity to better get to know her.

"This isn't me. I don't disappear like this," I quickly reply.

What Hadley doesn't know about me is I'm the reliable one, the good son, the one who doesn't take anything to chance. I guess the loss of a friend can change your prospective on life and have you making choices that may be frowned upon. My father will never understand that Hadley provided me with an escape I couldn't turn away from.

"That may be true, but things change—God, people change. That shouldn't define you. We all need an outlet, and you, Sean, are no different."

I can't speak. She is amazing.

How is it, this girl I have only just met can see me in this way, but no one else does? All I can do is stare.

"Your cell is with your clothes on my sofa. I put my number in it while you were using the bathroom last night. Don't lose it."

And then, just like that, I'm being dismissed. Turning back over, I watch as Hadley pulls her bedding up to her chin and closes her eyes. Pulling her door shut as I leave, I move toward her living room to retrieve my belongings. What I wouldn't have done to meet this girl when we first moved to Brooklyn. She is definitely a girl I could myself falling for if we ever had the chance.

Checking my cell, I can confirm that yes, I am in trouble, *deep trouble*.

I silently say goodbye as I let myself out of Hadley's apartment, willing myself to move to where I have been instructed to meet my family.

It's time to face the music.

CHAPTER TWO

TODAY

"I think I'll go," I declare loudly, to no one in particular.

Currently, I'm in Hawkes's communications room, going over the intel he has given me for our next mission.

"And where would that be, son?" my father responds almost instantly.

"Soph wants me to come out west. I think I'll go," I tell him.

Lifting my head, I focus my sight on my father, only to find him watching me intently in return. He will be wondering why the sudden change since every time he has brought it up previously, I have ignored him, changing the subject.

Before, I believed that losing myself in my work was all I needed, but I was wrong, because right now, my head is not where it should be. It's nowhere near where it should be for a guy in my position, or the missions I find myself a part of. By now, though, it's not just my father staring at me, it's Hawke as well, and I don't like how it's making me feel.

Why are they staring at me like that, like I'm under a microscope, some kind of organism for them to study?

"I think that's a wise idea, Sean," Hawke finally voices, breaking the silence.

He is still watching me, but not as stringently as my father.

"Why now?" my father asks.

That's a fair enough question I guess, but I don't know if I can answer it honestly. I don't want to admit that what I really want is to go back to Brooklyn and find a certain brunette? A girl who, for a short period of time, took away my pain and gave me respite from my demons. If I admit to that, there will be no way he will let me leave. Technically, my eighteenth birthday is still a few months away, which has him still trying to instill some authority when he can.

Unfortunately, I see him as nothing more than a hypocrite.

You can't enlist your fifteen-year-old son to help with dangerous government missions, teach him to handle all kinds of weapons and then try to enforce discipline.

It doesn't work.

I don't understand how he expects me to take him seriously.

If I tell him I'm going to Sophie's, I can detour to Brooklyn on the way. A distraction is definitely what I need, but my sister is not the kind of distraction I am chasing. Surely, my father can understand that, but I know he won't.

"It's time, and I'm no good to you as I stand today."

Now that, he will understand because it's time for me to say goodbye. Now that the dust has settled, it's time to finally let Sherilyn go.

"I'm sure your intentions are not as clear as you would like us to believe, but I will grant it."

See what I mean, he is trying to insert some authority.

"You would like to travel alone, I assume?"

Shit yeah, I want to travel alone. I don't want anyone knowing what I'm up to.

"Yes."

"Make the arrangements then." And then he is dismissing me.

Although I've seen flashes, I wouldn't say my father oozes any of the gentleness that my mother does. I've always found him to be more of a harsh, cold shell of a man.

And generally, a man I despise.

Without responding, I rise and leave the room. There is nothing more to say, so I guess it's time to contact Soph.

Me: *I'm heading your way.*

That's the message I send to my sister, moments after returning to my room. Logging onto my laptop, I search for flights. Hawke will have to transport me back to the mainland, but the rest will be on me. I will only need an overnight stop in Brooklyn before continuing to the West Coast.

Sophie: *About time!*

No phone call? I'm disappointed in that sister of mine. I was sure she would try to call.

Maybe she's busy?

Ah fuck, that's put shit in my head I didn't need. Now I'm thinking of her and Ben, and that's definitely not what I want in my head right now.

Me: *See you in seventy-two hours max. Something I need to do first.*

She will get it. She knows me better than anyone, always has.

Sophie: *No longer or I tell Dad.*

Bitch!

Sophie fucking would too!

Didn't I tell you she knows me too well. Although she won't know what I am up to, she will know it's not something I'll want my parents discovering. Sophie will assume it's a girl I'm going to see, but she won't know who. I've never mentioned Hadley to anyone; she's been my secret to keep and not someone I have wanted to share.

> **Me:** *See you then, Soph. I've missed your ugly face. :)*

That will amuse her.

> **Soph:** *You too, goose boy. Got to run. Have a date with a hot body ;)*

Yep, now I'm fucked. I really didn't need to know that shit.

Pinching the bridge of my nose, I throw my phone beside me to run my hand through my hair before continuing my search for flights. If I can get Hawke to take me, I can be on a flight by tomorrow night. I don't know whether to contact Hadley or just show up. She did, after all, give me her number, but for all I know, she could have moved on by now. Anything can happen in ten months. I know I should've tried to contact her sooner, but I didn't see the point.

When I walked out of her apartment that day, I swore to myself that I would never go back. I lied when my father drilled me, telling him that I spent the night wandering the city. I doubt he believed me, neither him nor Hawke, but they said no more, allowing me that privacy. My sister, on the other hand, was harsh, very fucking harsh. All her pent-up frustration, grief, and hurt was directed straight at me and rightly so. I deserved everything she spewed, for nothing more than I didn't tell them I was okay.

I didn't think, that much is true, about what my disappearance would do to my family.

It didn't matter to me at the time. My demons were being silenced, and just for a few hours, I was happy.

Booking my flights, now that will be the easy part, finding Hadley, unfortunately not so. I've thought of using the agency's assistance, but I won't. It will get me caught. I am going to show up on her door and hope she doesn't slam it in my face.

Now to speak with Hawke…

My senses have been on high alert since we landed in Brooklyn ten minutes ago. The flight itself, well, that was nothing memorable. It wasn't till we hit the terminal that everything started flooding back. It's way too fucking hot in here, it's making me dizzy. As if sensing that I'm going to pass out, I grab for something to steady me.

"Are you all right, son?" the old man behind me asks.

Shaking my head, more so to dismiss my dizziness, I smile and continue walking out of the airport terminal.

My first stop will be the Brooklyn Bridge.

Why?

Well, because that's where my parents, Sophie, Stephen, and the others decided to scatter Sherlyn's ashes. I chose to stay out of any decision-making, believing at the time that it wasn't my right to have a say. Obviously, my sister objected, but I'm more stubborn than she will ever be, so I won that fight. Ironically, the place that was chosen to release Sherlyn's ashes was near where I met Hadley. I remember thinking at the time, that just maybe it was a sign. I wondered if that was Sherlyn's way of trying to make me see what I had found and, in turn, was walking away from.

I even considered making contact before we flew out that night, but I couldn't. What would I say? *Hi, it's Sean. Bye, I'm leaving tonight.*

Yeah, that's real classy.

At that time, it was easier to walk away, but over the past ten months, it has gotten harder. She has been a constant in my thoughts, whether I have wanted her there or not.

Time to sort that shit out.

I won't make the same mistake twice.

Arriving at Hadley's apartment after saying my goodbyes to Sherlyn, I'm actually nervous.

Scrap that, I'm fucking petrified of how this is going to go down.

Knocking, I stand back a little. It'll make it easier to escape if it all goes to shit or if she no longer lives here. When the door opens, I'm hesitant, and she blinks twice before acknowledging me.

"Sean?" she questions, her eyes now wide and her voice full of surprise.

I guess after not hearing from someone for ten months, showing up unannounced can cause that kind of reaction in a person. Without words, she gestures for me to enter and turns away from me.

Following, I close the door behind me.

I'm actually surprised she didn't close the door on me after the way I left, but here she is, standing in front of me in her kitchen. She is once again waiting on me to say or do something.

"What is it you want from me, Sean?" she demands finally, breaking the uneasy silence that's settled between us. "What is it that you need from me?"

"I want you to take away my pain."

My voice is broken and distraught. Even I can hear that.

"I can't remove your ghosts, Sean. Only you can exorcise them. You are the only one who has the ability to lay them to rest."

How is it that this girl sees straight through me, and what is it about her that has brought me back here?

"I'm nothing more than a drug to numb your pain, but even you must realize the effects of what I can give you is going to be short lived."

Lying seems pointless, especially when my reasons for being in Brooklyn were to say goodbye to Sherlyn and find the girl who has been haunting my dreams.

"You have been in my head for months, Hadley," I confide.

My head is already lowered, my eyes firmly fixed on her tiled floor. I can feel her gaze burning into me, but I can't bring myself to look up.

"When I am at my lowest, it's your face I see, not hers. Tell me why that is."

"I can't answer that for you. Only you know why you are truly here."

Maybe it's the free spirit surrounding Hadley that makes her so damned adorable, or her honesty. My mother would like this one. She is very philosophical like my mother and Sophie. It's what makes them stand out, what makes them unique.

"I thought I knew what I wanted, and then Sherlyn died and I met you. It hurts my head wondering if I would be this drawn to you if she were still alive."

If Sherlyn were still alive, the chances of us meeting would have been nonexistent, even I know that, but I have thought about what my life would have been like if Hadley had been a part of my life prior. It's funny how you notice the little things. While I should be gazing into those beautiful eyes that suck me in, my vision is still fixated on her tiles, or should I say one in particular. Her kitchen floor isn't what I would call dirty, but there's a coffee stain I'm concentrating on at the moment.

Feet approaching snaps my attention back to the now, to her.

Stopping in front of me, she makes no attempt to touch me, simply holding her ground. Not much scares me, but the tense moment I find myself in right now scares the absolute crap out of me. Slowly raising my head, I keep lifting until we are eye to eye. Her stance is casual. Rven with her arms firmly crossed over her chest, those beautiful eyes of hers only reflect gentleness and concern.

Neither of which I deserve.

Somehow, the perfect ring from the splattered coffee on the floor beneath me is more settling than the position I find myself in.

"We would never had met. You already know this. Our paths would never have crossed, this I am certain of."

Yeah, there's that wordy shit I expect from my mom. She is right, though. I would not have been in this province had it not been for Sherlyn dying.

"Everything happens for a reason, Sean. Of this, I am a firm believer, and I was placed in your path for a reason. Nothing happens by chance. Everything is part of a bigger plan," she tells me, placing her palm to my cheek.

Her touch is soft and warm and makes me melt into her. "You have also plagued my dreams, lover boy. Come sit down."

Dropping her hand, she breaks the connection, thus destroying the moment. I flinch when she grabs my palm and slowly leads me to her sofa. Am I that vulnerable that even the slightest touch makes me jumpy, or is it just this girl? Her mere touch sends lightning bolt tingles through my every nerve ending. The beat of my heart increases as her fingers touch mine, my cock screaming to be set free. The effect she has on me is instant and unexplainable, but exactly what I need.

When I am in Hadley's presence, it's as though no one and nothing else exists. She was right when she said she was my drug. I know the fix is only temporary, but I crave her and the relief she brings, which floods through my veins.

I can only be here for the night, and I plan to spend it drowning in her body.

If she will allow me.

Without removing her hand from mine, she uses her other one to touch my cheek again, pulling me closer until our faces are inches apart. Her breathing picks up, matching my own as we rest our foreheads together. With my eyes closed, I drink in her essence, the wonderful smell of roses drifting from her body.

"I want you so much, Hadley. I need to lose myself in you," I admit. "Your hold on me is frightening. You know that, right?"

She giggles at my admission, and I can feel her body shuddering as though it's freezing. "I've missed you so much, Sean. Explain to me why I would be feeling like that after one night."

Whoa! Now I wasn't expecting her admission to match my own. I've missed every little thing about this beautiful girl in front of me, but I thought my feelings were a rebound thing. I never imagined she would feel the same.

"I'm sorry I didn't contact you," I blurt.

More admissions.

"I could have called you as well. This isn't all on you. I kind of stole your number when I gave you mine."

Opening my eyes, I see she is already looking at me, a smirk planted firmly on her delicious lips.

Cheeky bitch!

Sitting up straighter, I return her smirk with one of my own before demanding, "Bedroom, Hadley, now."

Her face registers the shock that my brashness has caused. My smile widens instantly. Saying nothing, she regains her composure and stands, moving quietly toward her bedroom. Just briefly, she glances back over her shoulder at me before continuing. I don't know whether it was to see if I was following, and don't worry, I will be soon, or if it's because she couldn't believe I just said that.

Removing my shoes, I leave them beside her sofa before making my way toward her bedroom. I want to build anticipation, but in reality, I could get in there to find my forwardness has amounted to nothing. Taking the risk, I throw my shirt and crap near my shoes and make my way down her hallway, leaving me in just my unbuttoned jeans. I'm hard as fucking stone and have been since she touched me in the kitchen.

I need to get my cock out of these confines, and soon.

Approaching her door, I'm hesitant, although I shouldn't have been, because the sight before me has me drooling. Hadley has stripped completely and is lying back on her pillows, legs spread, with her fingers rubbing circles around her clit.

Fuck me, this girl is hot.

"You are good at staring, lover boy, but how about you come over here and finish the job I've started?"

How the fuck can I refuse an offer like that?

"Are you as wet as you look?" I drawl, attempting to cover my own shock.

"You're extremely confident for a boy who let me have his virginity, aren't you?"

I shouldn't be surprised she picked up on that. I've no doubt I started out like a bumbling schoolboy last time we were together. I certainly didn't finish like that.

"Maybe," I drawl in return. "My teacher was good at her job. Maybe I now want to show her how quickly I learnt those new tricks."

My response makes her giggle, which is exactly what I was hoping for. "Well then, come show me how much you remember."

Another offer I can't refuse.

The whole time we were talking, her fingers never left her clit, and my eyes never left her fingers.

"I don't know, darlin', watching you touch yourself is fucking hot. Maybe I am happy just doing that," I tease from beside the bed.

Her eyes are closed, and a beautiful flush covers her face. "Keep up with that dirty fucking mouth of yours, and maybe that's all I'll want you to do."

Like I said, fucking hot!

I desperately need to remove these jeans of mine; the confining space is fucking killing me and my aching cock.

"What do you want, Hadley?" I all but whisper. "I know what I want, and that's for you to come all over those fingers of yours."

My words are obviously getting the better of her.

"Pants off, Sean—now," she demands. "I want your hand on your cock. I'm not coming unless you are."

Well, fuck me. If that wasn't a reason to strip, I don't know what would be. I can't get the remainder of my clothing off quick enough, slightly regretting wearing jeans at all.

"Unless it's on you, it's not happening," I taunt in return.

She's close, like real close, her thighs spread as far as they can go, as I move onto the bed. I come to a stop between her legs, and my hand pumps the fuck out of my cock in time with her fingers.

"I don't give a fuck where you put it, just do it. I can't...oh fuck," she screams.

Her scream triggering my own orgasm, my release spraying endlessly over her body.

"Fuck, Hadley, what the hell are you doing to me?" I breathlessly call out.

My whole is body shuddering in pleasure. Opening my eyes, I look at the mess I've made on her body.

"I could ask you the same question, Sean," she finally rasps, our breathing almost in sync.

"Shower with me," she suddenly demands, moving away from me, off her bed toward the door.

Turning her head slightly, she adds, "You can join me, or would you prefer to watch instead?"

I love watching her, I won't deny it. Everything about this girl is perfect. I need to savour as many images of her sweet delectable body as I can to store in my memory.

"I'm making sure I have enough images of you implanted in my head to feed my need."

"So when are you leaving again?" she asks, giggling at me as she enters the shower.

I so should have seen that coming.

"In the morning, so give me something to really remember you by."

Moving the curtain aside, her grin widens, drawing me to her, coercing me to get in. My cock already likes what it sees, hardening quicker than I expected. Giving in, I push off the frame and move toward her.

The hot water on my face is refreshing, washing away the last few months of worry. Hadley's wandering hands caressing my body doesn't feel too bad either.

"I love how you feel, Sean," her silky voice soothes from behind. Her body is squished against mine, her tits pressed firmly against my back.

My cock has been hard since I entered the stall. The sparks shooting throughout my body every time her fingers brush over my hardened length coax deep moans out of my mouth. She has me begging, "Fuck, babe, grip my cock. Your hands feel fucking amazing."

I'm already resting my palms against the tiles to steady myself, but her grip has my knees buckling. It's fucking blissful.

"I have a better idea," she says, turning me around.

As she falls to her knees, I think *Fuck yeah!* And memories of how hot her mouth was coming flooding back. There is no way I'll be turning that shit down. Gripping her hair, I yank her head backward so she can see my eyes.

"I want you looking at me. I want to see you sucking my cock."

Grinning, she accepts my demands, allowing me to keep my fingers entwined in her soft curls as she takes my cock into her mouth.

Oh my god, she feels so fucking good. That mouth of hers is so fucking wet and hot. There's no subtlety to her movements. She is sucking my cock like a woman possessed. If she keeps up this pace, I'm not going to last.

Throwing my head back, I release my grip on her hair, placing my hand instead on the tiles beside me to keep from falling. When I thought she couldn't possibly get any better, she starts sucking slower, more determined and even harder. I hadn't realized that she wasn't using her hands until her fingers encase my balls, massaging them.

Goddamn, she is fucking good at this.

Her fingers ever so slowly slide past them, moving upward until they are working their magic on my ass. With my senses already alerted, they go into hyperdrive when she manipulates one or two of her digits up and down the crack. Involuntarily, my hips thrust forward each time she gently runs them over the one place no one else has ever touched. I'm losing myself to her touch, all thoughts gone; just the pleasure of what she is doing remains.

My fucking god, she is good.

My balls tighten as the pressure of my orgasm starts to build.

As if sensing I'm close, Hadley picks up the pace once more, and I can feel myself slipping. Her hand is happily caressing my ass, and as I reach that point of no return, she slips her finger inside me. I've never imagined ever letting anyone touch me like that. Before I can think, my orgasm starts spiraling uncontrollably throughout my body.

"What the fuck," I scream as it takes control, flooding every inch of me with the most powerful sensation I've ever experienced.

My whole body tightens before it relaxes, and I realize that Hadley's finger is gone, her mouth full of my release.

I look down to find her extremely pleased with herself, grinning at me. "You are so fucking amazing. I have no other words," I blurt, kneeling in front of her.

Gripping her cheeks tightly, I smash my mouth to hers, allowing the need to consume her to overtake all other senses. I don't care that my release is on her lips. I just find myself desperate to taste her.

"You're not so bad yourself," she tells me once I break away from her.

Leaving the stall, she informs me that she needs food. Wrapping the towel around her body, she blows me a kiss, inviting me to take my time. I'm still sitting on the floor of her shower trying to catch my breath. It's going to be real fucking hard to leave her in the morning, but I don't have a choice.

My sister will make sure of that.

As I make my way to the kitchen, the smell hits me before I catch sight of her. It's becoming a habit for me to stand back and watch where this beautiful girl is concerned. The sight before me now is nothing short of breathtaking. All she has on is the shirt I discarded on her sofa, which just barely covers her ass, but fuck, it looks good on her. I doubt she is wearing anything else if the towel hanging over her dining chair is any indication.

Dropping my own towel, I grab my sweats out of my backpack. I didn't bother with a suitcase, especially since I wasn't planning on staying anywhere for too long. Throwing my towel on hers, I creep into the kitchen, stopping inches from Hadley, waiting for her to notice me.

"Sean, you dick," she screams, finally realizing I'm there.

Laughing loudly, I scoop her into my arms and kiss her lips. She wraps her arms around my neck, and I'm loving the feeling of her tits squashed against my chest. That gets an instant response from my cock, which is eagerly anticipating the warmth he will be heading into soon.

Gripping her ass cheeks, I lift her so that she can wrap her legs around my waist. "I think someone wants to play, Hadley. He always wants to play when you are near."

Her body shudders, and my cock twitches more at the realization that she wants me just as badly.

"Eat food first, then you can eat me later," she drawls, her pained voice matching my own as she slides down my body.

"Fuck, Hads, you're killing me here." I groan, my cock aching with need.

"All in good time, lover boy." She laughs.

Backing away, I sit on her stool as she places a plate of bacon and scrambled eggs under my nose. Taking a deep breath, I inhale the delicious smell from the food I'm about to ingest.

"I love the nickname," a gentle voice beside me whispers, making me smile.

Eating in silence, I devour what she has cooked, hungrier than I originally thought. Every now and again, she sneaks a look in my direction, no doubt thinking I'm not noticing. The problem is, I take notice of every little thing this girl does.

She is slowly becoming an addiction for me.

CHAPTER THREE

HADLEY

The incessant buzzing of a cell has me stirring. I've no doubt it will be my padre. It always is. A warmth next to me reminds me that I am not alone.

Shit…Sean.

My padre knows he is here. That's what the early morning call will be about. Sitting up, I attempt to shake the grogginess away. It was a long night, and I'd rather not be awake right now, but I suppose I should mentally prepare myself for the conversation I'm about to have.

That boy lying in my bed has stamina. He kept up with me all night, both of us crashing when we couldn't take anymore. The reminder of his touch, and that cock of his, sends shivers throughout my body. Unfortunately, a final fuck won't be happening, as once I answer my padre's call, I won't have long to get him out of my apartment.

I will worry about how to get rid of him once I have made my call.

Predictably, it doesn't take long for Padre dearest to answer. "Hadley, explain to me why that boy is with you."

"Well, fuck me, hello to you too, Padre," I grunt in return.

"Watch your mouth, child. I am in no mood to deal with your bullshit today."

Yeah well, I probably deserved that, but you must initially have respect for someone to give a shit about how you speak to them. It will be a cold day in hell before I respect that asshole who calls himself my father.

"Just spit it out. I have work to do."

He's quiet suddenly, but that means fuck all where Jason Alexandria is concerned. He will just be plotting how to discipline me, especially since I've been caught fucking the enemy again.

"I want that boy out of your fucking bed within the hour or he's dead."

I knew he would have eyes on me.

There is always someone watching.

I'm never alone.

And as per usual, he gets in the last fucking word before hanging up on me. Padre or not, he is the biggest asshole I have ever known. My problem, though, is that I'm his second in charge. My life hasn't been my own for years.

Now I need to get rid of Sean without raising suspicion.

Walking back into the room, I find Sean already up and dressed. He is fucking gorgeous, especially first thing in the morning. Those combat boots he is lacing up only complement the package I'm watching from the doorway. I can't help the pull between us, but unfortunately, we are never going to be more than this—a quick fuck when he comes to town.

Memories of what we have been doing all night flow through me, causing an ache between my thighs. For a boy with no experience whatsoever, he learns pretty damned quickly.

"You watching me now, Hads?" he grunts, a smirk brightening his face.

It throws me. I wasn't expecting him to see me ogling him. "Of course, it's my turn to save images to keep me warm at night."

The look he is throwing my way disturbs me, because it feels as though he is struggling to leave. The look is fleeting, but it was there, and it troubles me.

I need for him to leave; otherwise, my padre will have him killed, and that is something I can not allow to happen.

"I will be back, Hadley," he declares, his voice now serious.

He has risen from the side of my bed, stalking toward me with determination in his stride. Gripping my cheek with one hand, he roughly slides it down my face to lift my chin. Sighing, I turn away. I can't deceive him anymore, especially not now that I am developing feelings for him.

Fuck, what am I saying? I started developing feelings for this boy the moment I brought him home that first time, almost a year ago.

"Tell me what's wrong. I'm not leaving until you do," his soft voice murmurs.

He's so close to me now, his mouth gently brushing against my ear, and it's pure torture. I want him again. I don't think I will ever get enough of him.

"You have to go, Sean. You are in danger if you stay here," I admit unwillingly.

I am going to have to be honest with him, but once I am, I will never see him again. It's not something I want to happen, but if I don't, I will get him killed. Sean is the one thing my padre and I have fought over during the past year, and I refuse to back down. I have promised to give my all and do whatever was needed of me for the family business, on the condition that Sean stays alive and safe.

"I'm not who you think I am."

I hate it when he breaks the contact, moving away from me. The cold air that brushes past us as he steps back sends a chill down my spine. The expression on his face is darker now, colder somehow, and I expected it, but not so quickly.

"Talk, Hadley, now," he finally demands, and I release the breath I am holding.

It's now or never.

"We don't have long, so please just let me finish before you walk out of my life forever," I start.

He just stares at me, his face void of any emotion. Walking toward him, I hastily place my hands on either side of his face, pulling him in so that I can take one final kiss from his lips. He is going to hate me after I tell him everything, and I miss him already. Taking a step back, I lean against my doorframe again, watching as he crosses his arms, glaring at me. I was the only participant in that kiss, but it was enough to quench my need of him, for now.

"I am part of the Alexandria family, Sean. Jason is my father."

The look on his face is hard, and he is pondering, that much is obvious, as I immediately continue, "I am my father's consigliere, his right-hand man you could say, and have been for the past couple of years. I knew who you were that day on the waterfront. I was sent to kill you."

His eyes widen at my admission, and why wouldn't they? It's not every day someone throws an admission like that your way. Turning away from him, I step toward my window. With my back to him, the words keep flowing like I have no control over them.

"When I found you, I wasn't expecting the instant connection between us. There was something about you, and I couldn't go through with it."

There is nothing but silence behind me. I can't even be sure he is still in the room. I'm not a girl who fears much, never have been. Being a part of the Alexandria family expels fear from your bones from an early age. The expectations imposed on you from that early age are unrealistic, but you are forced into their way of life and eventually, you yield.

"Sean," I call, reluctantly turning.

There is nothing but silence, because he is no longer in the room. I shouldn't be surprised, but I am.

I never got to finish my story, my explanation.

SEAN

I couldn't get out of Hadley's apartment quick enough. Of all people, I had to find a girl who was part of the one family we are trying to bring down. As sick as it seems, I did find comfort in the fact that she was given the task of ending my life but had chosen not to. I have never been more thankful for anything than I was in that moment. God knows how long she had been watching that day on the waterfront. She could have done anything to me, and I would never have seen it coming. That was how fucking out of it I was.

Sitting under that same tree right now, I can't say my head is in any better place than what it was the day she found me. With my knees drawn, I'm just staring out at the water, contemplating what the fuck I have gotten myself into.

Is it just me, or do I attract trouble? Because it certainly feels that way.

Nothing about the last couple of years has been easy for me, and what makes this worse is the realization I came to last night—the one where I was falling for this girl.

If it wasn't already obvious, I'm well and truly hooked. Her touch had fed an unquenchable need in me all night long; she became my life support. It was as though nothing else mattered. Our only concern was each other's bodies. Every time we found our release, the simplest of touches refueled the kindle, reigniting the fire between us.

Regardless of all that, the realization that her father knows who I am now means I'm going to have to tell my own father about her. If they are on to me, they will be aware of him as well.

But I should have stayed and heard what else she had to say. All I heard was *Alexandria*, and I knew I had to leave. She is her father's right-hand man, thus being a part of what happened to Sherlyn. That alone should have me running back to my father, but that's not the reason I left. I got out quickly due to the threat of my life being in danger.

How selfish does that make me?

I have to get to Sophie. My head is a mess. I need to sort through the overload of information that's been thrust upon me.

Standing, I stumble toward a cab. If I can just get to the airport, I will call that sister of mine and make sure she and Ben are waiting for me. The vibration in my pocket surprises me. Grabbing my cell out, I'm stunned. For the first time since we've met, Hadley is messaging me.

> **Hadley:** *I'm sorry, Sean, this wasn't how I wanted you finding out. There is so much I need to tell you. Please don't leave yet. Meet me somewhere. I promise you'll be safe.*

Against my better judgment, I know I'll go to her. I won't be able to stop myself. It's not like I have anywhere better to be. My flight doesn't leave for a few hours.

> **Me:** *Where?*

She replies quicker than I expect.

Hadley: *1110 Manhattan Avenue. Meet me in the garden at the back.*

Shoving my cell back in my pocket, I give Hads's directions to the cab driver. If I'm correct, our destination is an Italian café my mother found when we first moved here. This whole situation is becoming very surreal very quickly. Resting my tired head on the leather behind me, I calmly close my eyes. You would think that I should be anxious about what I'm walking into, but I'm not.

I don't know what it is about Hadley, but as the cab driver approaches our destination, I feel as though I can trust her.

CHAPTER THREE

HADLEY

I *wasn't sure if he would come.*

Hell, if I were him, I wouldn't.

After all, I have been deceiving him.

I've known who Sean was for over a year now. I was given the task of getting to know everything about him when my padre's goon, Vincent, decided to chase that poor girl. I tried to tell my padre what he was doing, but he wouldn't believe me.

Well, he didn't until I brought him evidence. Only then did Padre dearest pay any attention. By then, though, it was too late, that poor girl was dead, and Vincent was eliminated.

You would imagine that holding the position I do in our organization, it would grant me some kind of authority, but you are gravely mistaken. My padre may take my concerns under advisement, but he holds all the cards.

Oh, but don't worry, I'm not one to be underestimated. When the situation arises that requires my unique talents, I can be one scary bitch, especially toward those who truly deserve it.

Like Vincent fucking Salvatore.

I grew up fast.

You fucking well had to in our family.

By the time I was sixteen, I could shoot, fight, and fuck as good as any man, if not better. There was no girly shit in our house. You learnt quickly how to fight for survival, and only the strongest succeeded—hence, how I got as far up the food chain as I am today.

Nothing was gifted to me. I earned my stripes, and it would be a cold day in hell before I would allow anyone to tear me down.

Until about a year ago...

When my padre's number-one hitman, Silo, was killed, I watched as his previous employee Vincent Salvatore sleazed his way back into my padre's good graces. If the whispers of gossip are true, my padre turfed his ass over a decade ago. That in itself is saying something because my father is the biggest fucking piece of trash to walk this godforsaken earth.

To say I hated Vincent was an understatement; I truly despised him. He only had to walk into a room to make my insides cringe. I kept telling my padre that his whole image was bad for our reputation, but he wouldn't hear anything of it. The guy had a crooked smile with yellow teeth for fuck's sake, and don't get me started on his balding head. Ugh, he was one of those dirty old men that you hear people talk about.

Yes, he was that bad, and I don't think I have hated anyone more.

Silo, on the other hand, I loved. His appearance was always immaculate, everything about him calculated. There was an order to him that I admired. He took the time to teach me just about everything he knew, letting slip once that I reminded him of his own figlia.

Everything he used to tell me, I absorbed. I was like a sponge, and when he died, I was devastated.

I loved him that much.

My own padre, well, that's another story.

After Silo died, my padre activated the clause, the insurance policy he puts into all his contracts. I tried to talk him out of it, especially after the madre committed suicide. I even came close to convincing him, until Vincent got in his ear. I don't know what he said or did to worm his way back into my padre's life, but whatever it was carried some serious weight. Knowing my padre, he probably had something on him. Little did I know at the time, Vincent had a motive behind his actions.

What surprised me the most was the girl's madre. I was astonished at what a waste of space she was. She had me in disbelief that a woman could be that much of a selfish bitch.

Who leaves their figlia behind for the circling vultures to swoop on?

I did everything in my power to deflect my padre's attention away from her, but I was fighting a losing battle, unfortunately. I believed that there was no point pursing the figlia since the madre was already dead, and I pushed my opinions onto him strongly.

The madre would have always been my preference anyway, just solely because of the way she treated her girl. Oh, and the fact that she let Vincent between her legs.

That in itself was a sickening thought.

Sean, though, now he became an obsession of mine. Around the time Silo died, my father pulled me away from the money-laundering scheme I had going on with our Swiss bank accounts. I channeled it through so many different accounts that no one cared by the time it reached its final destination. Most of the money I laundered that way was for Silo. He wanted me to set up a trust fund of sorts for his figlia, in the event that anything was to happen to him.

It was ingenious really. He scrambled the letters of his figlia's name to come up with a pseudonym, an alias so that no one would connect the dots.

Until Sean Valentine came along.

Fuck, that boy is good, but I know for a fact, he hasn't unscrambled the final pieces of the puzzle yet. For now, that's an advantage I still hold. It's the one link that can tie us to Silo, or so he believes.

A reflection through the glass doors catches my attention. Shivering, I wrap my arms around my body, fending off the chill from the breeze that's swirling around me in this garden court-yard. I specifically chose this location because it's my favorite and the last place I know that my padre would think to look.

Every morning I come here so that Mrs. Zegarelli can make me her famous hot chocolate. She is one of those old Italian-type women who loves to cook and talk. I do love the serenity that her café brings, and the books. Oh my god, I love the range of books she keeps here. It's like walking into your own personal library.

As the door creaks open, I spin around and freeze, watch-ing as Sean makes his way to me. It's the first time since I made contact that I have felt nervous in his presence.

"Spill," he flatly declares, his voice void of any emotion.

I know I deserve this cold, hard version standing before me, but I hate that it's come to this. Originally, I only wanted him for one night, to have a bit of fun and remove my obsession with him. I had every intention of fulfilling my padre's wishes once I was done with him. What was the harm in a little fun before getting down to business?

He was supposed to be nothing more than a job for me, a contract, a key figure my padre wanted eliminated. Only, once I was with him, and started talking to him, I couldn't do it. There was an attraction between us that neither of us could deny.

You're probably wondering how I can be this callous, considering I speak of taking another's life as though it's not that big a deal. What you don't understand is this is how I have been raised. I've pretty much had a gun thrust in my hand no sooner than I learnt to walk. I became my padre's figlia.

"It's not a short story, Sean," I counter, trying to hide the fear from my voice.

I've never felt this way before; this is all new to me.

"I've got time."

His glare troubles me, and I really don't like the idea of him being angry with me, even though I know I deserve it.

Sighing, I delve into my story, pacing back and forth as I speak. Part of me needs to keep moving so I don't have to see the disgust in his eyes, and the other part is trying to keep warm. I knew I should have grabbed my jacket before I left my apartment.

Starting from the beginning, I tell Sean that my padre is Jason Alexandria and my madre is a whore. By that, I mean she works in one of his whorehouses, a part of his prostitution ring. He once told me that he never saw the point of marrying because he didn't want some needy bitch stealing his money.

Imagine his surprise when I came along.

My madre also gave him a figlio, who is a year younger than me and one of his soldiers. Gerrick is working his way up to captain in an attempt to make our padre happy. Once he had a figlia and figlio, he never touched my madre again. I believe his words were that he "put her out to pasture."

He is such an ignorant fucker.

Over the years, I have wished to end his life, to make him pay for the miserable quality of life he subjects my madre to. Although there have been many opportunities to stick a knife in his heart, I've always chickened out because his death would only devastate both Gerrick and my madre.

There was a time when I too loved him unconditionally, but not anymore.

Finding courage, I swallow the lump in my throat and turn to look at Sean. He is by now seated in one of the outside chairs just watching me. His arms are crossed, but there isn't any malice in his stance.

Just curiosity.

It is like he is intrigued with my story, hanging on my every word.

As I begin to relax, I open up about my relationship with Silo and what happened to his figlia. I know her name but tell him that I believe it to be disrespectful to speak, as she is dead because my padre failed her. He allowed a madman to manipulate him, and because of that, an innocent girl suffered.

That was the particular moment my eyes were opened to the way of life I had become accustomed to, and I didn't like what I saw. I've killed and watched others do the same, but not once has it affected me to the extent that this did.

I admit to Sean that I know no other way of life, that both Gerrick and I grew up within this family structure, with very little outside influence. Killing became second nature to me, and I was fucking good at it. I learnt to shut off my feelings and concentrate on the job because that's all it was—a job.

During the whole time I spilled out my story, Sean never once interrupted. He sat quietly, listening to me ramble on, allowing me to continue. I feared that if I stopped, even momentarily, I would lose my courage and shut up.

When I got to the part about him, I found it amusing to see his ears perk up. I smirked as he raised his brow slightly. As much as it was killing me to admit, I had to tell him that he was originally a job to me, only later becoming my obsession. The fact that I knew more about him than he obviously liked was highlighted on his face, but he didn't stop me. I loved the fact that he just let me talk.

I love him.

There, I've admitted it to myself.

I love him and have done since I found him sitting alone on the waterfront. It's why I chased him, asking him to come meet me here. I found the strength I needed in his silence, and with that strength, the weight holding me down was lifting. I suddenly felt lighter than I have in a very long time.

"Where are we supposed to go from here, Hadley?" he finally asks, breaking the uncomfortable silence that had fallen around us.

His voice might have been small, but it was strong and determined. I know that makes no sense, but I expected so much more from him, and yet there was no anger in his tone. I think that's what has surprised me the most.

"You're not angry?" I ask in return, my voice full of surprise.

His eyes widen but only briefly. Washing his hand over his face, he looks up at me with the cutest puppy-dog eyes.

"I want to be, Hadley. Everything in me tells me I should because I loved Sherlyn, but I just don't feel it. Maybe it's because I love you more."

If I was shocked before, it has nothing on what his admission has just evoked in me now.

He *loves* me.

The grin that spreads across my face is uncontrollable. When I asked him to meet me, I never thought I would hear those words spill out of his mouth, especially after the story I had just spieled before him.

"Say it again, Sean. Convince me that I didn't just dream you said that," I croak.

My voice is sore from talking so much, but it matters not as I watch him stand. Cautiously, he takes tiny steps toward me, his eyes drinking in my body as he gets closer. The look in his eyes is heated, capable of melting me from the inside out, taking away the coldness from standing outside. Pulling me into his embrace, I place my cheek on his chest, closing my eyes to soak in his warmth.

"I love you, Hadley," he says slowly and meaningfully.

I could feel the sound of his voice reverberating throughout his chest before the noise and words escape his mouth.

Now what do we do?

"I love you too," I reveal, not wanting him to leave me again.

"Come with me," he whispers into my hair.

"Yes..." I breathe.

CHAPTER FOUR

SEAN

Never in my life have I ever been more serious about something than I am right now. Against my better judgement, I came back to Brooklyn for her, nothing else, just this girl in my arms. I wasn't joking when I said she was my lifeline, and every poor judgment I make from this moment on will be because of how much I love her.

The voices in my fucking head are screaming at me right now. They want me to leave, run away, and never come back. They are telling me to leave Hadley behind because she will bring me nothing but trouble.

I know it's the right thing to do, but I don't think I could leave her, even if I wanted to. The way her body feels crushed against mine has my cock straining behind the material of my boxers. It wants inside her even more than I do.

Regardless of all that, it's the feel of her heart against mine, beating rapidly, that has my blood pressure accelerating. We need to get out of here. Both of us should get moving before her father finds us.

"We need to leave, Hads. If your father finds us together, we will both wind up dead."

The sudden coldness that covers my body as we break our embrace sends a chill through me. Her face is beautiful, and the soft glow of her cheeks only accentuates her beauty.

"Not right now, lover boy. We need to plan. If I run now, my father will find me before I can safely escape. If that happens, he will have you killed, and I can't let that happen."

Fuck. That's not what I wanted to hear. All I want is for the two of us to run away, somewhere that we can't be found, but I know she is right. Her father would track us before we could get out of the country.

"We need a plan, Sean. We need money and a foolproof escape. I know my father better than anyone. He will not let me go easily. I'm in too deep."

Beautiful and smart, but I already knew that.

Pulling her into me one last time, I breathe her in, taking in as much of her scent as my senses will allow. I don't know when I will hold her in my arms again.

"You need to leave now, Sean," she murmurs into my chest. "Don't come back here," she scolds, pulling away from me once more.

The tears in her eyes break me. I thought I could feel her sobbing in my arms.

"I will come to you. I will find you."

Why does this feel like goodbye?

Kissing her forehead, I murmur "I love you" into her hair for the last time. I turn away from her and move toward the door. Her sobbing is loud enough for me to hear, but I can't look back; otherwise, I won't be able to leave.

Once again, I can feel my heart breaking, only this time, it's being ripped from my chest and Hadley is stomping it into the ground. There are easier ways to be rid of someone, and in this moment, I would prefer that she had placed that bullet in my skull after all.

"Sean, talk to me. You have been walking around here like someone broke that stupid Xbox of yours."

Huh! What the hell is Sophie on about?

Glancing up, I give her a puzzled look to find her staring at me. Her eyes are shadowed with worry, and I'm starting to regret coming here. I've been home, *or what was once home,* for three days now and have taken to spending my time on our balcony overlooking the ocean. I've always loved it out here. Apart from the peacefulness, the crashing of the waves below is tranquil and helps clear my head.

"Soph, I haven't used a gaming console in forever. What the hell are you talking about?" I sigh in resignation.

I hadn't realized I was that obvious. I'd been daydreaming about Hadley and have been the whole time.

"You, dumbass, have been moping around this house since you got here. What's up your ass?"

Screwing my face up, I take notice of what a fucking charmer that sister of mine has become. Living with Ben and the others hasn't helped her vocabulary all.

"Bottling up shit isn't good for you, Sean. You will end up exploding, and if you even think of directing any of that shit at me, don't. I'm not yours or anyone else's personal fucking punching bag."

Wait, w*hat?*

"Sort your shit out or go home. We've all worked too hard to move forward with our lives to have you bring us back down."

Nice! Real nice. Even Sophie is on my fucking case.

"I'm not bottling shit up, as you so charmingly put it, I said my goodbyes prior to flying out here."

I know my voice is harsh because even I can hear it, but I'm tired of being treated like the charity case.

"Maybe I have other shit on my mind and needed time away from the parentals."

The look she gives me is comical. Being the smart-ass my sister thinks she is, she would have thought she had me all worked out, yet she is wrong.

There was a time when I felt freer, when I enjoyed hanging out with the guys. Unfortunately, I'm not the same person and don't believe I ever will be again.

"Then what you need to do is open up to someone, Sean. I can see that whatever is going on is torturing you," Soph counsels, her face still radiating the worry I know she is feeling for me.

"I don't know what I'm doing anymore, Soph. My life has become more complicated than I ever imagined it could," I start to admit. "I've met someone. Actually I met someone months ago, someone that means a lot to me."

I stifle a smile, choosing to look away from Sophie instead. Her mouth is gaping, and it's fucking funny. It's the first thing since I arrived here that's actually made me smile.

"I'm glad I amuse you asshole, but how, when?" she snarls back at me.

That's the one thing I've always loved about my sister, her fight and determination. She has always been the stronger of the two of us, even though she would disagree.

"Sorry, sis, but the look on your face is funny. How could I not smile at your reaction?"

Her whole face brightens, the smile taking over, shining, relaxing me enough to tell her my story.

Starting from the beginning, I admit that I met Hadley the day Sherlyn had died, when I was at my lowest. Her face made me smirk several times when I gave her more information than she was chasing, but it felt good to finally get it off my chest. The relief that flooded through my veins was exhilarating and what I fucking needed. All my grief and guilt over Sherlyn's death flowed through my words, and yet Soph said nothing. She did for me what I did for Hadley, and that was allow me to finish, uninterrupted. I couldn't have loved my sister more than what I did in that moment. When I was finally finished, I sighed in relief.

"What stopped you from chasing her?" a sullen voice from behind me asks.

In the chair beside me, I hear Soph gasp, and it probably should alarm me, yet it doesn't. I may not have realized that Stephen was standing there, but I'm not disturbed by it either. If anything, I'm actually relieved. Pausing briefly, I take a moment to gather my wits before turning to get a good look at him. I shouldn't be surprised that his face is much paler than I remember, really ashen in color. His stance against the wall is that of a tired man, *a broken man.*

In the whole time I have been back, we haven't said much more than a grunted hello in passing. None of that is on him, though; it's all my doing.

Don't get me wrong, he has tried, but I've just felt the need to wallow in my own self-pity. I'm good at avoiding people, limiting my contact so that I don't have to deal with anything I can't control. Since arriving here, I hadn't considered the effect my morbid state of mind would have on the others in the house.

"A ghost," I finally reply, holding his gaze.

The words flow from my mouth in one shaky breath, a breath I didn't realize I was holding onto. Nodding, he slowly pushes off the wall to take the seat in front of me. I wish I knew what words would help him, although I doubt Stephen would listen anyway. He prefers his life of misery as much as I do.

"That ghost will be pissed that you let this girl go. You know that, right?" a steely voice directly aimed at me speaks.

He avoids the fact that Sophie is sitting beside me.

"Shit, she will be just as pissed at me for moping around as well, but I get it. I really do," he continues, stopping only to run his hand over his face, into his hair, in frustration.

"About fucking time," I hear my sister whisper quietly.

I doubt Stephen heard her, which is probably a good thing. Knowing Sophie, she would have been on his case as well. I know that he has been spending a good amount of time locked up in this house.

"From what you've just spilled, she had nothing to do with our girl's death. That is her father's doing, and I have no doubt he will pay for that crime."

Damn right he will.

When I spoke to my father after leaving Hadley that day, he promised me he would do everything in his power to eliminate Jason Alexandria. I listened as he expressed his disappointment in my actions and the subsequent hiccup I had now caused. I knew we were on their radar, but I never suspected that I'd been made a target.

My head hasn't been right in months, which meant errors were bound to happen. I think what surprised me the most were his words before I hung up—"What matters most is the lives of our children. What is important to you and Sophie is important to us. Bring Hadley home, Sean. Let us meet the girl who has captured our son's heart."

Remembering where I am, I catch the end of what Stephen was saying. "Don't punish his daughter for trying to prevent the inevitable. That fucker was never going to stop until he got what he wanted."

Stephen has caught me by surprise, and I have tears in my eyes. More words of encouragement from the unlikeliest of sources has me accepting what I need to do now. What I need to do is head back to Hawke's and plan what our next move will be.

"I don't know what I was expecting, but this wasn't it. I've missed you, man. I'm sorry I disappeared on you." The words just stumble out of my mouth.

My sister's comforting hand on my back startles me, but no more than Stephen pulling me in for a suffocating bear-like hug.

"Missed you too, brother," was all I got in return.

I don't think any further words were needed as he slaps me on the back and backs away.

Noise from the doorway brings me back. Looking up, I see Ben, Kyle, and Luke standing by the glass, cheering.

"About time, fucker," Luke calls out over the noise. "Glad to have you back."

It's good to be back.

CHAPTER FIVE

HADLEY

My padre knows something is up, but it's nothing more than suspicions he has at the moment, which I am fucking grateful for. When I allowed Sean back into my bed, I royally fucked up, and my padre knows it. I can't believe I was so stupid, but it's what that boy does to me. He unintentionally rips my guard down, causing me to act carelessly.

I, of all people, know that I need to be more conspicuous. I knew, the moment I let Sean into my apartment, how damning it would be, and then I had to go and allow him back into my bed. I knew he would have been watching, but at the time, I paid no thought to it.

There has always been someone keeping tabs on me, running back to him to try and crush me. Since the Sean incident—*his words, not mine*—he's been watching me even closer. I haven't been able to go anywhere without one of his men shadowing me.

Usually, it's my fratello, but more often than not, it's been that sleaze Luca. That asshole is one of my padre's captain and has been trying to fuck me since I turned sixteen. Every time I turn him down, it pisses him off more.

Unfortunately for me, that's the one my padre wants to marry me off to.

Yeah, I don't think so. It will be over my dead body that you will see me married off to some aging, sleazy fuck to keep the family happy.

I was fucking devastated the day Sean left. It took everything in me not to run after him. Yeah, I believed at the time that we probably could have stayed hidden for a while, but in the end, my padre would have found me.

I spent hours, after he walked away, just sitting toward the back of *Milk and Roses*, reading, drinking the endless supply of cappuccinos Mrs. Zegarelli placed in front of me. She never said a word; she just kept replacing my empty mugs until I'd had enough and was ready to go home. That's the one thing I've always *loved* about that woman; she knows what you need without ever having to ask.

To keep him safe, I haven't tried to make contact with Sean since he left. I know that if my padre gets any clue we are in contact, he will kill him.

There will be no threats made, of that I've already been warned. He promised that they would find him and shoot him— it's that fucking simple.

Once padre dearest was happy with the knowledge that Sean had left Brooklyn, he removed me from the job I had been working on—Sean being said job—and put me to work overseeing his brothels instead. I know why I have been placed here. It was punishment for disobeying him because he knows how much I hate watching my madre whore herself to the highest bidder every night.

To him, personally, she is worthless, but to his business, she makes him the most money each night. For a woman in her fifties, she still looks good, and he exploits that. Her olive complexion and soft brown hair give her an exotic look, driving the numbers up each week. This job will be the death of her one day, but she won't stop.

She loves him that much.

"Hadley darling, what troubles you?" my madre asks as she enters my office.

I shut myself in here when I first arrived, shielding myself from the senseless slavery my padre commits in this building. I have Maria to take care of the day-to-day *shit* out front. It's more her thing anyway. She's in her midtwenties, with tits that fall out of her too-small corset tops. She is all curves that girl, and the men love that. Add a bubbly personality and business is booming.

I have always found my madre's voice to be sickly sweet and loving—you know, like a normal madre's voice, and although I don't doubt she loves me, it's just not the way I need her to. If she did, I wouldn't be sitting here working on my plan to kill off the head of the Alexandria family.

Her love of that man and the choices she has made since brought both me and Gerrick into this world and into the life of a narcissistic control freak.

"Nothing that would concern you, Madre," I snap at her in return.

Her shift here at my padre's more elite brothel started a couple of hours ago and will finish somewhere around dawn. Night after night, she opens her legs, allowing a string of men between them without question or complaint. I've never understood how she didn't grow tired of it.

I'm happy to admit I love sex, especially when I am experimenting, but I couldn't live the life she has all these years.

"Since when do you treat me with such disrespect?"

Looking up from my keyboard, I find it amusing that she's attempting to fight back. Normally, this would be considered a good thing, as it would mean that some kind of emotion is finally starting to seep through the void behind her eyes.

"I've never had any respect for you, Madre, only ever tolerance."

I know that gets her since I don't hear the door shut as she leaves the room. With her gone, I can concentrate on the best way to remove my padre from his throne without drawing attention to myself. If I do it, I will be hunted for the rest of my life. I need to find a way of doing it and disappearing without a trace. Gerrick is going to be my hurdle as he idolizes our padre. This life suits him. He is more like my padre than I would like to admit.

Picking up the burner cell I purchased months ago, I type in Sean's number. A one-off message won't draw the attention of my padre since he is targeting phone calls between our other numbers. He isn't as smart as me; he's still very old-school.

Me: *Get a new cell phone. Call this number. Hads xx*

I'm hoping he responds. Every move we make now needs to be like a chess game, carefully thought out and one step ahead of my padre. Although I don't want to give my padre any reason to suspect the number I'm using, I need to be smart about what I am doing. I'm positive they are still watching the Valentines as much as they are watching me. For now, though, I think it's best we travel down this path, just because I don't want to imagine how I would feel if my padre actually followed through on his threat.

CHAPTER SIX

SEAN

Why does it feel like months instead of weeks since I last saw Hadley? Maybe it's because she haunts my every waking moment. Each memory that floods my head always involves her touch, hardening my cock instantly. I've never felt a need like this before, and since returning, I have been obsessed with finding a way to save her from her father without it involving a shootout.

Just after I returned from Solana Beach, I opened up to my mom, using her as my sounding board to work through my confusion. I think she was more excited that I was finally talking to her than about what I needed to say. When I headed back here, I wasn't sure what the fuck was going on with me. All I knew was this was the happiest I had been in a long time.

The final few days before leaving, I used my time reconnecting with Stephen, Ben, Kyle, and Luke, something that I desperately needed to do. I also spent a lot of time with Stephen, reminiscing, breaking down the wall of awkwardness I had constructed. I refused to allow it to stop me from spending time with the people I considered my brothers, my family.

The emptiness I felt after arriving back here dissolved quickly when their daily messaging started. Not one of those dicks were going to let me fall off the face of the earth again, and I was bombarded daily with an endless supply of crap.

I loved it, I won't deny that, as it brought a smile to my face every day. I've missed the hell out of them all. I just hadn't realized how much.

My cell buzzing next to me shatters my daydream. Thinking it was one of them, you can imagine my surprise when I swipe the screen and read the waiting message.

> **Unknown:** *Get a new cell phone. Call this number.*
> *Hads xx*

A surge of happiness suddenly floods through me. It's about fucking time she reached out to me.

Where the hell did Hawke hide those burner cells?

Searching the room, I find them neatly stacked in his cabinet with other weapons and accessories. You have to hand it to Hawke. He is ready for anything. *Well prepared* is the polite way of describing his communications room here in his fortress. Grabbing a cell phone, I check for charge before typing in the number.

"Sean," her sweet voice all but whispers.

Just the sound of her voice takes my breath away.

"Hads, fuck. I've missed your voice." I can't help but smile as her giggle echoes through the speaker.

"I've missed more than just your voice, lover boy, but soon, we will be together."

The smile on my face grows. There's my dirty girl.

"Oh, I've missed more than just your voice, babe. My cock has stopped talking to me in protest."

A loud eruption on the other end startles me until I realize it's just Hadley laughing out loud.

"God, girl, what the fuck was that? You scared the living daylights out of me for a minute there," I complain, causing her to laugh even harder.

"I'm sorry, Sean, but that was fucking funny," she stutters.

After she calms down, there is silence, which worries me. Is there someone there with her preventing her from talking openly to me? Wait, that can't be the case because she asked me to call.

"What's going on, Hadley? You asked me to call, and now you're not speaking to me. What's wrong?" Her sighing on the other end only heightens my worry.

"I'm sorry, Sean, it's just I don't want to be here, but I can't find a way out right now. My father is suffocating me with his presence. He is everywhere I go. I think he knows I'm up to something."

I need to step up my game and get her the fuck away from him, but how?

"I'm working on it, babe, just a little bit longer."

"I have to go, Sean, I love you."

Giving me no chance to reply, she ends the call, leaving me to the silence that has taken over once more.

HADLEY

Just the sound of my boy's voice was enough to entice just the smallest of smiles to my lips. Nothing of late has given me a reason to be happy, until now. I have missed him so much, and I didn't want to end our call so brashly, but I also didn't want my padre to catch me. It's like he has a second sense, choosing that particular moment to walk through my office door. I ended our call as quickly as I could, throwing my cell into a drawer with the hope he didn't see anything.

Slumping in the chair in front of my desk, I watch my padre as he says nothing, only eyeing me suspiciously.

Do I have a guilty look on my face, is what I want to say?

"What is it you want?" I ask, tired of the mindless head games he likes to play with me.

Nothing but silence greets my question, but I have come to expect that. It's always been a game for my padre, one that him drawing out the suspense in an attempt to use it as an intimidation tool.

I'll admit this may have worked on me once upon a time when I was younger and more impressionable, but not anymore. I outgrew his childish games a long time ago.

"Am I not allowed to visit with my only figlia?" he finally communicates, drawing out his words in a long, matter-of-fact, dull tone, the one he usually reserves for his enemies.

Now you would think that should raise some sort of alarm, but it doesn't because I don't care. Well, not in the way he is expecting me to anyway.

"If you want something, spit it out and then get out of my office," I reply flatly.

Regardless of his attempt I will not allow him to spark any kind of reaction in me.

That's the whole point of his visit right now, even I can see that. He no doubt believes I'm in need of some reasserting, and he believes he is the only one who can do that.

His response, which I know is meant to be threatening, booms and echoes throughout the room. "That's no way to speak to me, Hadley. Be thankful you are my figlia. Anyone else would be dead by now."

Little does he realize inside I am already dead. The only lightness in my life is thousands of miles away.

"Being your figlia means nothing. If you wanted me dead, it would have been done by now. I know what you did to *Nonno*."

That gets the reaction I was looking for. There is no longer a look of disinterest in his eyes, just a look of fear, which for a flicker of a second shines brightly.

And we are back to the silence.

"Tell me, Padre, when did you decide that *Nonno* had out-lived his usefulness, and are you not worried that Gerrick and I will do the same to you?"

Holding my statue, keeping my game face on, I watch as he visibly cringes.

"I'd ask how, but I can guess," he replies.

This time, there is nothing in his tone, no spitefulness, just a man acknowledging he's been beaten.

"How long have you known?"

He sits up straight in his chair, and the wall is back up. It's a self-defense mechanism of his that I have become accustomed to, as is the harshness he is now portraying. There is no gentle-ness to this man, especially when dealing with his own children.

"It doesn't matter how long. That information is irrelevant. Answer me. Why?"

It doesn't matter that I already know the answer to my question.

I am just trying to prove a point.

I watch as he straightens and takes me in, like really takes me in, as though I am now his competitor.

"Yes, the old man did outlive his usefulness," he starts.

Holding his gaze, I see nothing but blackness, a dark color that occupies his heart as well.

"I knew I was better equipped to handle the family busi-ness, so I took it from him. You of all people should understand how our world works."

Yes, I do.

I understand completely.

This world is the only one I have ever known.

I was born into a dark world of power-hungry, money-stealing murderers. My padre tops that evil list as the most power hungry of them all.

"What changed you, my angelo?"

Ugh, I hate it when he calls me that—his angel.

I haven't been that since he threw me out to the wolves when I was sixteen. That was the day the man I loved, the one I looked up to, became the man I *hated*.

"I changed, Padre dearest, when you whored me out to those Colombians all those years ago. I stopped being your figlia when I was sixteen years old, and I became a bargaining chip."

I was hoping for some kind of reaction when I threw that charming fragment of information in his face, but still nothing. My padre is nothing more than a calculating piece of shit, a man void of emotion, and no one is safe from him—not even his children.

"You used me back then to broaden and strengthen your hold on the market, for your greed."

I've read about these standoff moments in books. This is supposed to be the part when he begs me for forgiveness and wallows in his regrets. Unfortunately for me, that isn't going to be the case. The man who spawned me just stands and glares back at me with his cold black eyes. This is exactly what I expect from him.

"I made you the person you are today, my love. Don't forget that. You and your fratello are strong and capable of handling yourselves in any situation because of me."

And we are back to that again. I have heard that same spiel many times over the years, and before it would have had an impact. In the past, it always brought me back to him and made me feel guilty for attempting to rebel, but not today.

I am stronger *piu forte*, than I have ever been, and his words will not desecrate me. I watch as my padre moves toward the door, as if to dismiss me.

"You still haven't told me why you are here," I callously call out.

Slowing his pace, he turns slightly to engage me.

"I came to tell you, figlia dearest, that you need to stay away from that boy. He will be the bringer of death."

I knew he was here about Sean.

"Take care, mio angelo. I'll be seeing you real soon."

When the door closes, I slump in my chair and start to relax. It's always tense when I have to address my padre, and I can't wait for the day when I am rid of him from my life for good. Pulling the hidden cell phone from my drawer, I smile when a message from my love lights up the screen.

> **Sean:** *We will be together soon, beautiful girl. Remember that I love you.*

I know my smile is growing, but that's just what that boy does to me.

I can't believe I even contemplated killing him. Not that any of that matters anymore; my days within my padre's organization were numbered when I didn't pull the trigger. Bedding him instead only cemented my fate. Eventually, either he or Gerrick will be forced to take care of me, or I will have to agree to my arranged marriage. Neither of those outcomes appeal to me at all, meaning I am going to have to strike first.

> **Me:** *The sooner, the better, lover boy xx*

> **Sean:** *Why did you hang up?*

Fuck! I wasn't expecting him to still be awake.

Shit, I will need to find out if we are even on the same time zone.

I wouldn't imagine we are, but then again, I have no idea where he is hiding either. The only locations we have for the Valentines is their home in Solana Beach and the apartment they resided in here in Brooklyn. I didn't ask Sean where he was hiding because I didn't want to place him in danger if my padre tried to extract it from me.

My padre's interrogation methods are inhumane, and I should know. I have used them myself. The success rate for extracting vital information has always been extremely high, with no one ever lasting more than twenty-four hours.

Well, there was one. It was one of those Colombians who my padre whored me out to. Once he had his fun, I turned the tables on him and had some of my own.

I tied that asshole to the bed in the sleazy motel room he took me to and spent the next seventy-two hours perfecting my skills.

Unfortunately for him, he didn't survive, but I became a useful tool for my padre, bumping me up the food chain ahead of my fratello.

After that day, I never allowed anyone to walk over me ever again, and that included my padre. I'm just better at manipulation than the rest of his puppets.

My madre and fratello never understood my reasoning for such a drastic transformation, but I also never wanted them to be concerned for my well-being. I may be my padre's figlia, but I am smarter then he will ever be, and that will eventually be his demise.

His death, though, won't be as merciful as my beautiful nonno's.

Now that's a man I miss daily.

Don't get me wrong, he was a ruthless son of a bitch and a mean old bastard, but never toward his grandchildren. He and my nonna made it a habit of spoiling Gerrick and me, much to the irritation of my padre. When Nonna passed, he was never the same. She was his only love, and her death was a revenge killing.

My nonno had executed a Russian family in cold blood.

It was a vicious, calculated attack to take over their territory that bordered on our own. Nonno was all about expansion and wanted to have a majority claim on the drug trade. He succeeded, but it came with a cost. He lost my nonna and my *zia* in that hit, and it left him a broken man. That was when my padre and my uncle took it upon themselves to eliminate him, staking their claim on his livelihood, the foundation he built from the ground up.

A couple of years later, my padre's greed led to him killing my uncle as well.

What I don't think my padre ever expected was Silo filling me in on the gruesome details. He admitted to me one drunken night that he committed the hit on my nonno. He told me the burden of carrying it around all those years was too much to bear anymore. To say I was upset at first is an understatement, until he told me that my padre had originally organized for Vincent Salvatore to do it. Silo couldn't and wouldn't allow that to happen; his loyalty to my nonno was stronger than that of my padre.

One final thing he mentioned was that Nonno knew it was coming and had been relieved that it was Silo carrying it out.

He died quickly and peacefully.

My cell vibrating in my palm reminds me of Sean's message. As I type out my response, my head is still planning how to deal with Padre dearest. Something up close and personal is what really appeals to me.

Me: *My father was here. Please be careful. He knows I'm up to something. I will be in contact once I have fixed the problem. I love you xx*

Sean: *Be careful, Hads, I couldn't do another funeral.*

If nothing else, that message from Sean grounds me. The thought of not making it out alive has never occurred to me at all. I need to break away cleanly, but I can't do that without removing the one person who keeps me chained here. I am never going to be truly free until my padre is *morte*—dead.

Me: *I have no plans on dying, lover boy, but I promise I will be careful xx*

I just hope now I can keep my promise.

Turning the cell off, I slip it in my bag. I can't talk to him anymore tonight. It will only produce feelings of guilt, and if I am going to pull this off, I can't be harboring any of those kinds of feelings.

What I need to do is get my game face on. This family needs a new head, and my fratello is the obvious choice.

"Why are you still here, Hadley darling? You never stay for more than a couple of hours."

Putting down my pen, I glance at my madre, who has made herself comfortable in the leather seat across from me.

"As much as I despise what this building represents, Madre, I'm required to oversee the day-to-day operation."

Normally, I would have made my escape by now, so it pains me to see her this morning because I know the night has not been good to her.

She looks tired and worn, more so than usual. When I looked over the sign-in sheet I received from Maria an hour ago, I noticed that my madre was kept busier than usual.

"Why are you so mean to me, figlia of mine?" she asks, breaking our silence.

I don't mean to take my frustrations out on her, but I hate watching her waste her life like this.

Sighing, I push the sheet of paper in front of her. "Because of this, Madre, because you allow Padre to treat you like a piece of meat. I hate the way you let him manipulate you so that you'll sell yourself night after night for him to profit."

Slumping back in my chair, I sit and wait to see what lame excuse she comes up with for what she does. I know I have put her on the spot, forcing her to acknowledge the reality of her situation.

"This is all I know, sweet child," she quietly admits. "I love your padre dearly, and it's the only way I can stay close to him and my children."

Whoa, what the hell.

"I know you hate him, Hadley, that you hate the man he has become. Please understand he has not always been this way."

I know what she's trying to do, but she is wrong.

"How do you know that, and what do you mean it's the only way you can stay close to your children?" I accuse.

Honestly, how does she know that he wasn't just playing her?

Did he threaten to take me and Gerrick away if she didn't whore herself for him?

It makes no difference to me because from what I have observed over the years, my padre is a very good fucking actor.

"There are just some things you can't fake, my child." Waving her hands as if to dismiss me, she continues, "Forget I said anything about you and your fratello."

Laughing, I lean back even further. "You're naive, Madre. You can fake everything under the right circumstances." Straightening, I lean forward on my arms, taking her in.

"You can't make a comment like that and ask me to forget. I grew up around that man. I've seen it for myself what sort of a man he is."

She would never believe me if I told her, so now's not the time to speak badly of him.

"He has his faults, I'm not that blinded, but the man I met is not whom you see today. That is the man I love and always will. I am not going to speak of what I should not have mentioned. Please do not ask again."

There is no polite way of speaking about the man who told me when I was sixteen that I had to earn my place by his side. Her comment, though, has me thinking back to when I was younger. It's odd, but I never really noticed my madre's absence in the main house because she was still around.

When I became a teenager, I had questions that needed answering, and only my madre could answer them. I needed my madre, and my padre would only allow limited visitations with her. Even today I still don't understand why that was. Over the years, I just accepted that it was his way of controlling us.

Pieces of a very old puzzle are starting to come together, and it's painting a picture of what she must have had to endure to keep us close to her.

Isn't this all the more reason for me to put an end to his reign?

"As you wish, Madre. Live in your denial, but don't ask me to treat him any differently. In my eyes, he's not worthy of my love. If you knew what he has forced me and Gerrick to do over the years, you wouldn't be so defensive."

Sighing, she rises, murmuring "good night" as she leaves. I love my madre, but I won't sit around anymore watching as her life wastes away before her eyes.

Twirling my chair around to watch the sun rising through my window, I stare at the beams of light reflecting off the glass.

A quick glance down at my watch tells me it's nearly 7:00 a.m. This is usually the hour I find myself curled up on one of the sofas at Milk and Roses, drowning my sorrows with one of Mrs. Zegarelli's hot chocolates.

Every morning since Sean left has seen me follow the same methodical pattern, a trait my padre despises.

"*Predictability is a weakness,*" he always preaches. "*It is what will get you killed.*"

My padre will be the reason I get killed, not my predictability or my love of coffee.

"What's troubling you, Hadley?" a deep voice from behind rumbles.

Whatever thoughts I had are now shattered as I spin my chair around to the direction the voice is coming from. With visits from my padre, madre, and now my fratello, it's becoming a bit of a family affair today. Very rarely am I ever granted the privilege of all three of their presences in the space of twenty-four hours.

Now I know something is definitely wrong.

"Your visit, for one," I declare coldly.

Gerrick's eyes narrow suddenly, his lips tightening into a thin line. I have angered him, but I don't care. I refuse to allow him or my parents see any of the vulnerability I've been feeling lately.

"Why are you here, Gerrick?" I sigh heavily.

Frustration is creeping under my skin, and my patience for bullshit is wearing thin.

"Padre sent me. He is concerned about you."

And there is that bullshit I was talking about. I knew there had to be a reason behind his visit. Gerrick always texts me. He never just *shows up* expectantly.

"He believes your obsession with the Valentine boy is clouding your judgment. He doesn't believe your priorities revolve around the family business anymore."

Shit. I knew it!

"There is no obsession. He was just a *fuck*—a good one at that, if you must know," I reply with a smirk.

Watching my fratello screw up his face is priceless. That's what he gets for being a nosy fuck and my padre's messenger boy.

"Do you have to be so crass?" He sighs in return, pinching the bridge of his nose.

"Yes, because you and *Padre* have stuck your noses in my business for too long. If I want to fuck the target instead of killing him, I will. Whatever business we had with them died when Silo's daughter died."

Sitting back, Gerrick stares at me, trying to read my thoughts.

"I don't believe you, Hadley. You like this one. You may think you can hide it, but I know you better than *Padre* ever will. What I want to know is why? Why this boy?"

Leaning forward in resignation, I rest my arms on the desk in front of me. Closing my eyes, I pinch the bridge of my nose briefly, mimicking my fratello's previous action, before running my fingers through my hair. As my fingers pull at it gently, my head rests against my hand, forcing my arm to carry the weight.

Sighing once more, I open my eyes to see Gerrick still watching me, but now more intensely. I may be able to fool my parents, but I can't lie to my fratello. Our bond goes deeper than that. I won't allow myself to betray his trust.

"There is something about him that makes me feel safe, that makes me believe I can have a life away from the family," I reluctantly admit.

"When I'm with him, nothing else matters, and I want that, Gerrick. I want to be normal."

He just sits there, continuing to watch me, and for the first time in a long time, I'm actually afraid.

Finally, I watch as Gerrick leans forward and gestures for me to give him my hands. Reluctantly, I give in and place my hands in his. Compared to mine, they are large, with a roughness to them.

The texture of his palms, mainly the harsh feeling of them, reflects the type of work my fratello is involved in. Everything about his role is hands-on, which pains me, because the last couple of years have been no easier on him than they have on me.

"Then go for it, Hadley. Chase your dream."

Did I just hear him correctly?

Surely not, because that would mean my fratello, my own flesh and blood, is telling me to leave and escape.

"It's not that easy, Gerrick. You of all people should know this."

Grunting in what I believe is frustration, my fratello shakes his head.

"Nothing about our lives has ever been easy, but I've never seen you back away from a challenge before," he replies, pulling his hands carefully from mine to sit back in his chair.

"What's stopping you now?"

With his arms now crossed over his chest, I have to wonder if this is a test to see whether I'm still loyal to the family.

His face is stoic, giving nothing away, but I'm tired of hiding, and in a quiet voice, I concede. "There is only one way I'll ever be able to walk away, and that's if I end our padre's life."

Fidgeting, I twirl the pencil I've picked up, focusing my attention on the exit instead of Gerrick's face. "And I can't do that to you and Madre."

An admission such as the one I have just given should result in my death, and if that's what's to happen, then I welcome it. After the brief interlude with Sean, I know that I will never be the same person I was. I'm only fooling myself to think I can revert back to that cold, heartless girl.

"I want him dead as much as you do, Hadley. He needs to be held accountable for the sadistic things he has done to us," Gerrick quickly blurts.

The expression reflecting on my face surely was one of shock, especially after believing all these years that he idolized our padre. What surprises me the most is that my fratello feels the same way.

I've heard the stories over the years, rumors of the horrific things Gerrick has been subjected to, but he never speaks of it. Many times, I have tried to get inside his head, but he shuts me down and becomes distant.

"It's time for me to be honest with you, Hadley, and finally give you the answers you have been seeking."

CHAPTER SEVEN

SEAN

"Good morning, mother," I greet cheerfully as I enter into our kitchen area.

She is quietly reading her book at the dining table, sipping on the raspberry tea in front of her.

"Good morning, Sean," she beams back at me. "You seem happy this morning. It pleases me to see you this way."

A huge smile radiates on her face as she responds to me, "I've missed your smile, son." In that precise moment, I realize that I share her sentiment as well. I have also missed her smile.

"For the first time in a long time, I feel I have a reason to smile."

I haven't made the past twelve months easy on myself, but when I woke this morning, I was happy and full of hope for the future. I spent last night waiting up until I had a response from Hadley. Although I knew that the reality of our situation meant that her messages would be few and far between, I couldn't sleep until she had made contact. This girl I have found brightens my world, bringing in a lightness that I never thought could exist.

"I'm happy to hear that, darling. Is there any progress on your young lady's retrieval?" she asks, putting her book down to give me her full attention.

I love how she allows her glasses to sit on the bridge of her nose. It reminds me of a school teacher I adored in junior high.

"Not yet, but apparently, Hawke will brief me once I am finished with breakfast. I'm only getting limited intel from Hadley's end, so I don't know what is going on back in Brooklyn."

"Please be careful. I don't think this old heart of mine could handle any more tragedy," her now small voice pleads.

Placing my bowl on the benchtop, I choose actions over words. Walking up behind my mom, I place my arms around her midsection to embrace her. Kissing the top of her head, I promise to be careful. Releasing her, I move toward the communications room, where I know Hawke and my father will be waiting.

"Ah, there you are, my boy," my father hollers from his place in front of the multiple screens Hawke has installed.

For a man who was supposed to retire from the Central Bureau of Intelligence last year, he is still actively working as an agent. He works behind the scenes these days, mainly intelligence after opting out of fieldwork when Sherlyn died. At the time, he cited that he could no longer disembody himself from his work and his family. He believed his judgment would impact the missions and he would not be responsible for another death.

"Come see what we have discovered."

Taking the empty seat next to him, I look at the photo of Hadley on the screen.

"You're looking at the brains of the Alexandria family," he continues. "Jason Alexandria isn't going to let his daughter go without a fight. Are you ready to get your hands dirty?"

Why my father felt he needed to ask that question, I don't know, but shit yeah, I'm ready to get my hands dirty.

"What more have you uncovered? What's our plan?"

During the briefing with Hawke and my father, I learnt that Hadley Alexandria is, indeed, the brains behind the Alexandria family. She has been linked to racketeering, loan sharking, prostitution, murder, and pornography, and that's just what we know of. Her involvement in the sex industry is a concern for me, and the man in me is praying she wasn't in front of the camera.

If so, was it voluntary or forced?

When we were investigating them during the ordeal with Sherlyn, our main focus was on her father and Vincent. I knew that Jason Alexandria had a son and daughter but never really took much notice of those details. Up until just a few moments ago, I had never seen her photo in any form. She was never a concern for me.

My main focus was her father and the contract he had with Silo. Taking the file from Hawke, I excuse myself to retreat to my room so that I can read up on my girl in private. I'm under no illusion about what I will find; honestly, I'm expecting the worst.

Sitting back against the wall on my bed, I cagily open the file, and straightaway, I'm confronted with Hadley's photo. Everything about her face reflected in that picture is hard and guarded and not like the girl I have come to know.

Skimming quickly through the file, I find out that what they have on Hadley is a lot more extensive than I bargained for. It's also lot thicker than I was expecting, and by the looks of this, she has played an active role within her father's organization. I know I shouldn't be shocked, but her involvement in her family's business is greater than I anticipated. Whatever hopes I had of retrieving her quickly and without incident seem impossible now. My father wasn't wrong when he said we would have a fight on our hands. What doesn't help the situation is not knowing what's happening on Hadley's end and what she's doing to aid our mission.

Delving deeper, I'm starting to understand why I had so much trouble tracing the monetary trail. It appears that she was heavily involved in the racketeering side of the business. From what I've been reading, my girl is extremely successful at extorting money and finding ways of laundering it.

Over the past three years, through Hadley's involvement, her father's worth has increased by at least fifty million. There is no way he is going to want to lose her. The problem the CBI has encountered is, although they know what she is up to, they've never been able to arrest her. There is no actual physical evidence that can be tied back to her; she is that damned good at masking her activities. Everything they have on her is inconclusive and mostly word of mouth. People love to talk when money is thrown at them, and that seems to be the case here.

Unfortunately, that's not where her involvement seems to end.

Over the years, many have snitched or leaked information against her, but not one of them is alive today to tell their tale. Each and every one of them has been the victim of a tragic accident within days of passing on their information. Although there is no actual evidence to prove their theories, agents at the CBI believe the one and only link to their deaths is Hadley herself.

As much as I'd like to believe she is innocent of these accusations, I'm also not that naive or stupid. I have no doubt she played a part in their murders. After all, she did confess that I was meant to be one of her targets as well.

Regardless of what is written in this file, there will be no impact on how I feel about this girl. My own actions over the past couple of years have been questionable, to say the least. What I have to do now is converse with Hawke and work on a plan to bring Hadley here with us. How we are going to do that is a question I have no answer for right now, and our progress has been brought to a standstill as I wait on word from Hadley.

Grabbing the burner cell I borrowed from Hawke's stash out of my bedside drawer, I turn it on to check for messages. Waiting for it to turn on is having a nervous effect on me, as I wait and hope that she has sent me something. As the screen lights up, it doesn't take long for the phone to start beeping, and a smile covers my face.

Hadley had sent three messages:

> **Hadley**: *Hey, sexy boy, I'm missing you xx*

> **Hadley**: *I have news for you. I will phone you at 8 pm Brooklyn time.*

> **Hadley**: *Can't wait to hear your voice xx Love you!*

Shit, what time is it?

I wonder what the time difference is.

I didn't think of that, and to be honest, I have no idea. I guess I'll just have to leave the phone turned on until she calls. Throwing it beside me on the bed, I return to Hadley's file to see if there is anything in it that will help us plan her escape.

I can't deny I'm curious about the news she has for me. Maybe it will be something that will help us bring her home— home to me.

HADLEY

"Are you fucking with me right now, Gerrick?" I splutter in my *fratello's* direction. My voice coming across brittle, as I attempt to hold back my tears. I always knew that my asshole of a *padre* was just as tough on Gerrick as he was on me, but I never expected this.

"Yes, Hadley, now you can understand why I've never told you before," he replies, releasing an exasperated sigh, turning away from me to move toward my office window.

As he pushes the wooden frame outward, the brisk morning breeze filters in, giving this musky room a refreshing makeover. Leaning forward, he settles on the frame, allowing half his body to hang outside.

"Why have you not killed him yet?" I growl, anger now overtaking my tone.

Watching him closely, I stay standing on the other side of the room, near some boxes of paperwork. The fight to keep these tears of mine at bay is consuming me, making me too high-strung right now to even attempt to console him. He inhales a deep breath of air and returns inside.

"Because I was too young to take over and needed time to strategize. It's taken me a fucking long time to gain any respect among the men. I had to prove myself over and over to manipulate them. If there was ever a time to strike, that time is now."

"And strike we will," my quivering voice utters in agreement. "But right now, I need sleep, Gerrick, so meet me back here later, and we will discuss this more."

Knowing me well, my fratello simply nods and leaves me to my thoughts. It destroys me inside to turn him away with no words of sympathy, but he wouldn't have been seeking any either.

As he leaves, I can accept that he is right, but my mind is still reeling with everything he has finally confessed. I'm so angry with my padre, my hands clench tightly by my side. The likelihood of me drawing my 9 mm from my drawer and shooting him if he were to walk through that door right now is extremely good. Unfortunately, a bullet to the head is way too fucking nice, especially after what he has done to me and Gerrick over the years.

Gerrick's admission about what he has been through was honestly one I wasn't expecting, or even something I would have contemplated. I knew my padre was sadistic, but this goes beyond that, even for him.

When he whored me out to cement his hold on a bigger slice of the drug trade here in Brooklyn, he also did the same to Gerrick. Unfortunately for my fratello, he was unaware that he was the meat my padre was throwing to the lions.

"Padre's been whoring me out for years, Hadley."

That one sentence, Gerrick's admission, shocked me, and not just slightly either. It took me at least ten minutes to find my composure and my words to respond. During that time, my fratello took my silence as an invitation to continue. His story, compared to mine, was horrific.

Maybe I'm more like my padre, after all, as it appears my tastes teeter more on the dark side. For me, I used that moment to my advantage, giving me a better standing in our family hierarchy. Gerrick, on the other hand, simply toed the line. He allowed our padre to continue to use him and his body as payment in a bid to increase his stake with the Colombians.

The thought of how Gerrick could allow this to happen did cross my mind while he spoke, but it was like he was reading me. He admitted that the first time he fought against it, until they pumped a syringe full of cocaine into his veins. Everything after that was a blur. What he can recall of that night involved three Colombian men and a shitload of cocaine and booze.

By the time they had finished with him, he was that fucking high on coke he didn't know who he was or what was happening. The damage they inflicted on his poor body that night involved him being hospitalized with severe trauma. He didn't go into details, but my imagination had enough images running through it that I didn't need his words.

Thinking back to then, I clearly remember him being in the hospital, but my padre brushed it off as a gang hit and nothing more. If I had realized the severity of his injuries at the time, I would have made those men pay. I would've taken great pleasure in torturing them, but my own mind during that time was in a horrifying place where I thought of myself and no one else.

After that night, Gerrick admits to using the coke they supplied to help him escape while they had their fun. Engaging became easier, and eventually, it wasn't just the Colombians my padre whored him out to; it was anybody he thought he could manipulate.

The regularity is what sickens me the most.

The fact that Gerrick now enjoys it only saddens me. He declares that although he no longer needs the drugs, he still uses, and he enjoys the company of both male and female partners.

My fratello has become a goddamned drug addict, and I never noticed.

Obviously, it makes me wonder if this would've still been the case if he hadn't been forced into it. It's no secret that we've been surrounded by drugs our whole lives. Maybe he would have, or maybe he would've been strong enough to stay away like me. It really does make me a mixture of sad and angry when I think about what he has had to endure, regardless of the fact he now welcomes it.

My fratello's sexuality, well that has never been a concern to me, as long as his practices were safe. It's been no secret that I'm bisexual; in fact, it's a trait my padre often brags about, but I can't say I have ever picked up on Gerrick being the same. He has always been a very private person, especially when it came to sex.

To be perfectly honest, until moments ago, I just assumed he was still a virgin.

What angers me, the thing that has my blood boiling, is the fucked-up situations my padre has exposed him to. We may have been teenagers, the children of a self-proclaimed power player in the Italian mafia, but we were innocent.

The evilness that has always been buried deep inside of me wants to be set free so that I can dissect my padre piece by piece. I would love to release her and allow her to tie him down, putting our acquired knifing skills to good use.

There is also now another part of me that just wants to walk away and leave him to Gerrick and escape. The problem is, I just don't think I could do that, not after everything Gerrick has opened up about and confided.

I have to get out of here.

Grabbing my things, I lock the door behind me.

My brain is eagerly conspiring, excitedly creating options. I know my padre well enough to know he wouldn't suspect a thing. I can't image him ever believing that Gerrick and I would have the courage to harm him or rid of him in the same manner as he did our nonno.

The only difference will be that we won't be putting out a contract on him—the pleasure of ending his life will be ours. He wasn't wrong when he said we are stronger because of him, but that will ultimately be his downfall.

"Hadley child, wake up, dear," a kind, soothing voice swirls around me like an old comfortable blanket.

Dazed and confused, I wake with a start.

What the...

Where am I?

Oh, that's right. I'm at Milk and Roses, and it's Mrs. Zegarelli trying to wake me.

"Sorry, Mrs. Z, I didn't mean to fall asleep," I yawn.

Twisting my body around, I straighten my legs to remove the numbness of having them curled under my ass while I slept. I watch as Mrs. Zegarelli picks up the book I was attempting to read off the wooden floor and places it on the little coffee table in front of me.

Sitting herself in the chair across from me, she frowns.

The tired, aged lines across her face are all I notice as she says, "You work too hard for that padre of yours, my darling. You need to rest. A beautiful girl like you should be looking at settling down and marrying a wonderful man who will grace you with darling little bambini."

A comment like that I expect from the older Italian women. They are old-fashioned, their lives revolving around their demanding husbands and children.

I love the Zegarellis, I really do. They've always been here for me, allowing me to lose myself in the simplicity and wonder of their small Italian café.

What I am *not* is traditional.

I don't want to marry some aging captain from my padre's organization and hang around to cater for his every need. I want more than that life entails, more than Mrs. Zegarelli and my madre will ever experience.

"That's not for me, Mrs. Z, you know that, but thank you for allowing me to rest. I need to get to work now."

Rising, she maneuverers her way slowly around the coffee table to pull me into her embrace. Hugging me tightly, she kisses each of my cheeks before releasing me. Mumbling something in her Italian tongue, she heads back to her other customers, leaving me to gather my things.

Glancing back, I spend a few moments just watching her, marveling at how she carries herself. I spend an additional few minutes wondering if there will ever be a day when my life will be as carefree as hers.

Shaking my head, I turn and exit, heading back toward my padre's whorehouse and my madre.

Saying hello to Maria as I enter, I can't help but smile at her bubbliness. It doesn't matter what hour of the day it is, that woman is always cheerful.

Walking toward my office, my senses are overcome with a feeling of anxiousness, as though something is terribly wrong. Slowing my steps, I cautiously approach the door to my office, all the while cursing myself for not having any weapons on me.

It's so unlike me not to have something hiding on me, somewhere.

My hunting knife—my favorite weapon—is in my backpack in that very fucking room. My head was such a mess when I left earlier today that all normal protocols I follow were forgotten.

Reaching my office, the door is slightly ajar, making my stomach flutter nervously. Gently pushing it open, I step through the threshold, waiting for the ambush. What I encounter is not a welcoming sight, and confirmation that Gerrick and I need to act quickly as my time is nearly up.

"Beautiful girl, I've been waiting for you," a strident, unpleasant tone greets me.

I should've known my padre would send Luca to speak to me.

"What is it you want, Luca, and why are you sitting at my desk?" I grunt in return.

"Hadley, my darling, isn't it obvious? I'm here for you," he draws out, emphasizing the last part while leaning forward to lecherously gaze over my body.

Every goddamned time we are in the same room, his vision fixes firmly on my tits. I can't recall an occasion when his eyes weren't undressing me.

It has never mattered who was in the room, his eyes are never level with my own, and today is no exception.

"How many times must I tell you, Luca, if you want to talk to me, you need to look me in the eye. My tits aren't going to give you the time of day," my frustrated voice retaliates.

In my padre's organization, men like Luca are a dime a dozen. All of them are sleazy, egotistical bastards who believe women are only good for one thing—an outlet for their frustration.

After the Colombians, I never allowed anyone to touch this body of mine, unless I've wanted it, and Luca will never get his loathsome hands on me—ever.

"Ah, Hadley, would you really begrudge this old man the act of gazing on such beauty?"

Resting against the back of the chair he is seated in, he gestures toward himself, lowering his voice to a deep growl as he continues, "When will you give yourself to me and really experience the pleasure I can gift to you through pain?"

Ugh, just the thought of that makes me shudder.

His lust-filled eyes darken as his heavy gaze narrows in on me. I would rather die than let that shriveled-up cock of his anywhere near me.

"Gazing on my beauty and eye fucking my tits are two entirely different things," I chastise, placing my hands on the table.

Leaning forward, I thrust my chest toward Luca deliberately. I know I'm playing with fire, but acts like this are expected of me.

"Now once again, before my patience wears thin: What. Do. You. Want?"

Grinning, he rises slowly from the chair, placing his large hands near my own on the desk. There are tattoos across his knuckles that I have never noticed before—*sangue* and *family* (blood and family)—that distract me for a second, giving Luca the opening he needs to strike.

Before I'm fully aware of what's happening, both of my hands are gripped in his, forcefully yanking me down, splaying me across my own desk.

My head crashes down on top of the wood, hitting the edge, rendering me defenseless.

Dizziness quickly takes over, consuming my head and making it difficult to guage the situation I'm in. Sharp pain floods my chest like a hot iron, piercing my skin from when he slammed me down onto the hard surface. There's tightness suffocating my chest and pressure from something, or someone, holdng my body still.

Panic engulfs me as I struggle against whatever is restraining me, but my attempts of breaking loose are futile. More pain shoots through my head as I'm struck with something hard. Circles of darkness swirl around, pulling at me from every direction. They are dragging me under and swallowing me completely, forcing my already heavy eyelids to close.

Why is it so goddamned cold in here?

Grogginess clouds my head as I awaken, and I shiver because of the sheer coldness of the room. There is searing pain convulsing through my head, and suddenly I remember.

Fuck.

It's all coming back to me—Luca hitting me with something and knocking me out. No wonder my brain is so scrambled.

Attempting to move, I realize I'm bound, each of my limbs secured with thick rope. I'm guessing the rope is twisted around the legs of my desk because when I try to pull on it, I can't. He has my arms and legs tightly restrained. There's no movement at all.

Motherfucker!

Lifting my head as high as I can, I force it from side to side looking for my captor, and then it dawns on me. I'm cold because I'm fucking naked.

Luca has me stripped bare.

I'm spread-eagle and restrained across my own desk, and there's not a damned thing I can do to free myself.

"Oh good, you're awake, Hadley, finally," a deep, throaty voice drawls from somewhere behind me.

The lust in his tone is evident and it wouldn't surprise me if that sleazy fucker is sitting back, enjoying the sight of me tied down.

I know Luca well enough to believe he is probably fisting his pathetic excuse for a cock while he sits drooling over my naked *lily*.

"I'm sorry for the crude manner in which I have restrained you," he speaks once more. "But I came here to take what is mine and to also show you who is in charge."

Once again, *fuck!*

Struggling more, I continue to pull at my restraints in a desperate attempt to get away from Luca and the fucked-up spectacle he has made me the star of.

I don't like it, but he has me at a disadvantage, and I need to rein in the panic that is slowly swirling in the pit of my stomach. It's rising, seeping through every vein in my body at an alarming rate. I hate it, hate how this scenerio is hauntingly similiar to the one my padre subjected me to all those years ago.

"I'm here if you need me, Hadley," a soft voice echoes throughout my head.

"Don't fight it, angelo. I'm going to fuck your gorgeous cunt, and there is nothing you can do to stop me."

God, I wish I wasn't tied down.

Unfortunately, Luca knows how dangerous I can be, and he won't want me getting hold of a weapon to hurt him.

"I know what you are thinking," he voices, coming around the desk into my line of sight. "Because I know you, Hadley. I know what is going through that pretty little head of yours."

"You know nothing about me, Luca, and once I get free, I *will* kill you," I snarl.

His eyes widen, and the stunned look on his face causes me to smirk. My words have hit their mark. Lifting my head as high as it will go, I glare at the vile creature now sitting in front of me.

I wonder if he is game enough to come any closer.

Grinning, my evilness rises, and I'm imagining riping his balls from his body, using only my teeth. I'd be like a dog with a new chew toy, spitting them out when I lost interest in the old rubbery leather.

"Let me do it," that voice pleads.

"That's where you are wrong, my dear. I know you better than anyone, and I know exactly what you are capable of."

Replacing my grin with a scowl, I glare at him.

Standing, he takes slow steps, brushing his rough fingers over my skin.

"I have plans for this body of yours, Hadley. You have no idea just how hard the softness of your skin is making my cock," Luca breathes, his fingers digging deeper as he continues. "I've wanted to fuck you for too long, but all that ends tonight."

Fuck, fuck, fuck.

There's no escaping the inevitable.

Luca is going to rape me.

The bile in my stomach is rising, I can feel it. Fear raises its ugly head, moving out of the shadows of my mind, laughing at me for thinking I could ever be free of it.

When his fingers drag along my side, they dig into my skin, making me cringe as he progresses further down my body. His touch is making me physically sick, my whole body shuddering in disgust. When his hand finally leaves my skin, I have an overwhelming urge to vomit.

Luca's sharp intake of breath gives him away.

He's reached his destination.

Breathlessly, his words come out strained as he whispers loudly, "See, you like my touch. Why do you fight against me so much, Hadley? If only you would give in to this feeling, give yourself to me willingly."

Ugh, no way that's happening. He's fucking delusional if he thinks I actually enjoyed him touching me.

His lips touch my thigh, breathing his words across my skin, reverberating them throughout my body.

"I'll have you screaming my name by the time I have finished with you."

His actions surprise me, and my body jolts forward until I'm pulling against the rope tied around my ankles. Every muscle, whether used or not, is now burning, the result of being restrained for so long.

Pain viciously slices through me every time I try to move.

My body tenses at his touch, and any attempts to rein in my emotions aren't working at all as I try and regain what little control I can.

"I will feel no enjoyment, Luca, make no mistake about that. Every reaction you draw from me will be forced. My body will have no other choice but to betray me."

Paying no attention to my words, lust fuels Luca's movements. His palms grip the backs of my thighs as he drags his chair closer. The screeching sound of the metal legs scraping across the wooden floor boards echoes painfully in my ears.

Anxiousness continues to swirl, slivering its way up and around my body in its pursuit to strangle my internal organs. The sense of suffocation grips at my throat, making it harder to breathe, threatening to engulf me.

Shutting down, I can still feel Luca's touch, but it doesnt stir any reaction from me at all.

He is mumbling to himself words I cannot and do not want to hear. His breathing becames increasingly erratic as his fingers apply more pressure on my clit in his desperate attempt to make me orgasm.

Regardless of his intent, my body has stilled and is lifeless under his caressing hands.

The only feeling I'm succumbing to is the one of being detached from my body. It's as though I'm watching the lurid things Luca is performing on me from afar.

I can actually envision it all in my head.

When I hear his zipper lowering and the ripping of a packet, my panic rises to a new level. As I accept my fate, I can feel tears welling in my eyes.

This is really going to happen.

Luca is going to fuck me on my own desk against my will.

At least he has a minute amount of decency to use a condom.

I'd be lying I didn't admit that I would do anything to have someone burst in right now and stop him from defiling my body.

With my eyes tightly closed and my tears dropping onto the wood beneath me, I prepare myself for what is about to happen.

"Why won't you let me help you?" the voice deep inside asks of me.

Because you can't, I reply.

"Are you ready, my sweet? I tried to make it easier for you, but you've resisted. Now I'm going to fuck you anyway, and in any orifice of my chosing, until your body can take no more."

Curling my hands into fists, my tears continue to fall as he thrusts into me.

"Ah, beautiful girl, this cunt of yours is truly a remarkable thing," he grunts, withdrawing from my body.

He thrusts back in, even harder this time, the impact jerking my body forward—well, as far forward as these ropes will allow it.

The taste of bile sits at the back of my throat, and his continuous spiel of obsenitites is making it hard to suppress my need to vomit. The vile words spewing out of his mouth, and the continuous assault his cock is inflicting on my *lily* has me wishing he would just kill me already.

Death has to be kinder than what I'm being made to endure.

"Ah fuck!" he screams, his body jerking as he reaches his release.

"Exquisite, my dear. That tight cunt of yours milked my cock quicker than any of those whores your padre keeps locked up in this building."

Well, that wouldn't be fucking hard. I am at least ten years younger than most of them.

"Including your madre."

What the fuck!

Actually, I shouldn't be too surprised that he's fucked my madre; she is a whore, after all.

"Unlike her precious figlia, Melania loves to be tied up," he declares, stepping out from behind me, settling by my side.

Dropping his head closer to mine, whispering in my ear, he taunts, "And do know what she loves the most, precious one?"

His vicious words draw my attention even though I'm trying to ignore him. Standing up straigher, he's fisting his cock as he snarls at me, "Your madre loves it when I take this hard cock of mine and impale her ass."

Did he really just say *impale*?

I mean, seriously, who the *fuck* says that anymore?

If I wasn't terrified right now, I'd be laughing at him. Now, though, I have visions of him with my madre that I don't want and could've lived without.

I gulp, but there's suddenly no moisture in my mouth at all. The dryness of my throat is limiting my ability to swallow. It's becoming more of a luxury than a necessity at this point, and I hate to admit it, but Luca's words are finally having an effect on me.

My heart is pounding.

Drawing out just enough courage to put up some kind of resistance, I stutter, "Is t-that supposed to impress me?"

"It doesn't matter if I'm impressing you, sweet Hadley. That little virgin, or maybe not so virginal, hole above your cunt has been taunting me."

Creeping closer, he leans back down. "I will be burying my cock in there soon enough, and no resistance from you will stop that."

My face twists in a scowl.

Anger boils deep within me, overtaking any fear I had been feeling.

Rage bubbles, waiting for a window of opportunity to present itself.

"Just remember, Luca, whatever you do to my body will result in me inflicting ten times that pain in return. I will get free eventually. You can't keep me tied up like this forever."

"That may be the case, but for now, *I* am in control. Although the idea of you on your knees, bound like this in my basement, is a delicious thought."

The smirk on his face is sickening. He really is a sadistic fuck.

I've always known he had a taste for kink, but never this extreme. With the way the girls around here talk, you learn more about our clientele's preferences than you care for.

"Are you ready for me, angel?"

My earlier fear resurfaces, and my body tenses in preparation.

Panic grips me as Luca slowly takes his time, painfully scraping his nails along my body until he's standing directly behind me once more. One of his hands grips my ass, causing me to flinch when his fingers forcibly dig into my cheek. If his weight bearing down on me is anything to go by, I'm imagining him fisting his cock with the other. The grunts of pleasure now flooding my ears will prove to be confirmation of that.

Pressure from beneath, on my clit, startles me, my body jerking as his finger slides up along my *lily*, parting my lips. Sliding it inside of me, he curls his finger and drags it back in and out of me, digging his nail into my flesh, causing nothing but pain.

"I need you wet, angelo, for what I'm about to do, but you're not being very cooperative. Since you are working hard to fight against me, I'm done trying to make it easier on you. Time to take what has always been mine."

Balling my hands into fists, I brace for his attack.

The sound of another wrapper echoes in the silence.

I know he is still speaking to me, but I'm drowning him out. His voice is nothing more than a faint whisper ghosting around the room.

Instead, I concentrate on Sean, silently wishing that he was here with me. If I hadn't been so *fucking* stubborn, then Luca would never have gotten close enough to touch me.

If only I hadn't been so determined to deal with my padre on my own.

My thoughts drift back to my boy and how he is going to react when he learns what Luca has done to me.

The iciness within the room starts seeping through my skin, burying itself deep into my veins. As the coldness continues to overtake me, my body shakes uncontrollably. Scrunching my eyes tightly shut, I can feel the wetness as my tears escape once more, trickling down my face onto the surface beneath me.

For people like me and Luca, fear is a valuable tool.

It's one that I have used in the past to push my victims, breaking them down so they prayed for death, willed it even, to escape the pain I was inflicting on them. It's been a long time since it's been me on the receiving end, since I've felt the level of fear flowing through me in this moment.

Right now, I'm praying that Luca will just take out his gun and kill me.

Willing my mind to concentrate on anything other than what is happening, I try to shut out the ramblings of the madman attempting to *fuck* my ass. Pressing forward, I feel his cock traveling the same path as his finger. He pushes it up along my *lily*, parting my lips, briefly entering me before pulling back out and continuing to the "pot of gold at the end of the rainbow," as he so unattractively put it.

This is it.

There's no way out.

When he was fucking my *lily*, I could zone out and not allow myself to feel anything, because it was *nothing*. The thought of him readying himself to rape me anally, though, is *fucking* freaking me out.

This is something I won't be able to ignore.

The memories of the night my padre whored me out to those Colombians comes crashing back into my head, flooding my eyes with visions I thought I had buried. Whatever self-control I thought I had is now gone as terror rears its ugly head. It's grinning and laughing at my helplessness as it grips my insides, squeezing the life out of me.

Gasping desperately, I fight against the terror that's trying to crush my lungs. My heart feels like it's about to explode; the thumping vibrates loudly in my ears. Nothing, not even my violently shaking body, is going to stop Luca from taking what he wants.

With my focus soley on the fear that's consuming me, I'm oblivious to what Luca is doing until he thrusts into my *ass*. The pain is instantaneous, and it takes everything in me not to scream at the top of my lungs.

FUCK!

Laying my head to the side, I let my tears flow, biting down on my arm to suppress the *fucking* pain that's screaming throughout my body. I don't know if it's from the blunt force he used shoving his cock into my tiny hole or the rope that's cutting into my limbs after being forcably driven forward.

Embedding himself as deep as he can go, he stills, his fingers dig painfully into the cheeks of my ass. I flinch as a new wave of pain grips me, but this time, it's managable, nothing like the pain from him entering my ass.

"Oh, angelo, I knew your ass would be tight," his breathless voice exhales. "I'm going to enjoy fucking it often."

With raggard breaths, he begins to move again, sliding his cock out completely. Over his breathing, in the background, a click catches my attention.

"Step away from my sorella, Luca."

Gerrick.

My fratello is here.

"I don't think so, boy. It's you that needs to step away. Lower your gun and walk back out the same *fucking* door you entered."

The grip Luca has on me tightens as he addresses Gerrick. The tip of his cock rims my ass, sitting just outside as he prepares to slam back in.

"I don't think so, old man. Remove your cock from Hadley's body, or I'll shoot."

Gerrick's voice is hard and toneless, void of all emotion. If I could see his face, his eyes right now would be reflecting nothing but blankness, and his jaw would be set. It's a look I've seen many times before, right before he kills someone.

My padre created his perfect replacement, a heartless killer in the form of his own son.

"This body is mine, Gerrick, and you would do well to know your place." Luca barks at my fratello. "I will remove my cock from Hadley's body when I am done with it. Now lower your gun and leave."

Using this moment to enforce his authority over both of us, he shoves his cock back into my body.

Without any warning at all, a loud bang shatters the silence, and Luca's body falls forward, crushing me under his weight. All the air from my lungs exits my body upon impact, leaving me gasping.

"*Fuck*, are you okay, Hadley?" my fratello's concerned voice bellows in my ears.

Hurridly, he removes Luca's dead body from mine, and I finally start to relax. Cursing loudly beside me, Gerrick starts moving around the table, rushing to untie the ropes securing my limbs.

"*Fuck, fuck, fuck,*" he continues to curse. "You're free, Hadley. Let's get you covered up."

Lifting me off the desk, Gerrick carries my limp body over to the sofa. Laying me down, he covers my naked body with his jacket. I want to thank him, but my voice is lost, stopping me from saying the words.

Tears stream down my face as he comforts me, whispering over and over again that it's going to be okay.

Kissing my forehead, he tells me he is going for help.

I don't want him to leave, which he senses, but he reassures me that I'm safe. Just before he leaves, he looks back and tells me he will be back soon. More tears slide down my cheeks when I glimpse the sadness hovering in his eyes.

Turning away from me, I watch as he leaves the room, closing the door behind him.

Exhaustion is finally kicking in, and my battered body sinks into the cushions of this sofa. I succumb to the pressure and allow my heavy eyes to close, knowing that Gerrick will keep me safe.

Waking, my eyes open, but my vision is blurry. There's so much grogginess clouding my senses that it takes a few minutes to focus on my surroundings. The constant rhythmic beeping of a machine in the background gives my location away instantly. As I regain focus, it becomes obvious that I'm lying in a cold, sterile room, in a hospital bed. Beside me, my sleeping fratello is resting his head on the mattress.

He looks peaceful, angelic, *innocent*.

"Gerrick," I hoarsely croak.

I wait a few minutes, but nothing, he's not budging.

Sliding my hand across the bed toward my fratello, I lift it to gently stroke his hair. Not surprisingly, his hair is still as soft as I remember it being when we were younger, back when he used to crawl into bed with me to hide from the monsters.

Gerrick would curl up next to me, tucking himself under my arm. He used to make me stroke my fingers through his hair until he fell asleep.

I didn't understand at the time, but I do now.

One of the monsters he was escaping from was our padre.

Heaviness sets in, and a painful ache in my joints forces me to drop it back down onto the bed. Movement of my other arm only produces much of the same.

"Gerrick," I croak again, a little louder this time, and he stirs.

When he does wake, it takes him a few minutes to register his surroundings, and I watch as concern floods his face.

"I'm okay, Gerrick," I reassure him, sliding my hand over his in comfort.

The touch of my hand visibly relaxes him, and I smile when he grips tightly in return.

"He will never hurt you again, Hadley," he swears when he finally finds his voice.

It's tiny and much weaker than it normally would be, but he's wrong. It should be me protecting him, not the other way around.

"I'm just sorry I didn't get to you sooner."

"It's not your fault, Gerrick. You didn't know what he was planning," I attempt to voice through my croakiness.

Anticipating my actions, Gerrick brings me over a cup of water. Directing the straw into my mouth, he tells me to take small sips. The coldness of the water both cools and burns as it travels down the back of my throat.

"I knew he was up to something, though," he admits.

Dropping his head in guilt, I stay quiet and listen as he continues.

"I was summoned to our padre's side late last night under false pretenses. He apparently was concerned about one of the Gerabaldis and needed me to sort it out. I was halfway across the bridge when I realized I'd been set up."

"How did you know?"

The blue eyes looking into mine are not the ones I love. They are *haunted*.

"I knew"—he pauses, letting an exasperated noise escape his lips—"because when I asked which one, he said Joey."

Joey?

Wait, what?

"It wasn't until I was crossing the bridge that it dawned on me. Joey Gerabali has been dead for six months. I should know. I was the one who put the bullet in his head."

That motherfucking, worthless piece of trash. It's time for the two of us to finish this; otherwise we are both going to end up dead. Gerrick and I have obviously become too much of a threat for him to keep around any longer.

"I was on my way to tell you when I walked in on Luca attacking you." His whole body tenses at the memory, his hand clenching under mine.

Squeezing mine down onto his, I bring him back to me.

It's something I've always been able to do.

When he was little and something scared him, I would grab his little hand in mine and squeeze it tightly. It was as if he sensed I was there, snapping him out of whatever dreamlike state he was in.

"Sorry, it's hard to remove those images." Looking up, his eyes are wet with tears, and my heart breaks for him.

"After I killed him and made sure you had received medical attention, I went back to confront our padre. He sanctioned the attack on you, Hadley. Our own flesh and blood gave that monster permission to rape you."

Oh my fucking god, my own padre is the reason I'm in here.

"I wasn't suppose to survive, was I?"

Gerrick's silence confirms my suspicion. That bastard had used Luca to torture and rape me, the very same man he was trying to marry me off to.

"Answer me, Gerrick," I demand.

"No, no, you weren't," he whispers.

His voice is brittle, but it's the tears streaming down his face that make my heart ache.

I'm too shocked to respond. I knew my padre was planning something, and it was stupid of me to ever underestimate him.

"He wants us both dead, Hadley." Gerrick's voice snaps me out of my thoughts.

"He would've known what would happen the moment I stepped into Gerabaldi territory. They want revenge. I would have been killed."

I'm speechless. Everyone knew Gerrick was a target. Joey Gerabaldi's death caused more than just rumbling between the families; it caused a war. My padre's reasoning for that hit was sketchy at best and left his son with a contract out on him.

"I have made contact with our enemy. We need their help with this. Padre has his men close. He is expecting us to retaliate. I'm not proud of asking the Valentines for a favor, but it became a necessity."

He's contacted Sean?

"We will have reinforcements by sundown. Our padre is going to die tonight, Hadley, and I can promise you, it won't be quick or painless. Before the sun rises tomorrow, I will be the new head of the Alexandria family."

Still speechless, I just watch as my fratello rises from his chair and leans toward me. The tears trickling down my cheek as he kisses my forehead was unexpected and something I can't control, yet when he notices it, he just smiles.

Wiping it from my cheek, he pauses for just a second before leaving my hospital room.

CHAPTER EIGHT

SEAN

I can't help but wonder what the hell I've gotten myself into. When my father, Hawke, and I landed last night, Gerrick Alexandria was there to greet us. You can imagine our surprise when we found him sitting in arrivals waiting for us, especially since we hadn't made any prior arrangement.

For someone normally so composed, the sight we were faced with was completely out of character. Gerrick looked like shit, all disheveled and haggard, like he hadn't slept in days. Everything about his appearance screamed train wreck, right down to his fidgeting.

He couldn't sit still, and that concerned me. If I wasn't mistaken, Gerrick was coming down from something. I would've thought the risk it imposed on him by being seen with us would've had him being more discreet.

Although Gerrick is close to me in age, that's where our similarities end.

Hadley's brother has been groomed to take over for his father all his life. The file we have on him is not for the fainthearted. It floored me when I answered my cell a couple of nights ago to one of the more narcissistic members of the Alexandria family.

The only reason I answered the call in the first place was because I had been anticipating a call from Hadley. Her brother, Gerrick Alexandria, wasn't someone I ever expected to hear from, which is why my first instinct was to hang up. It was the fear in his voice that stopped me from doing that.

Gerrick was calling, looking for help. He needed our assistance to get rid of his father. Initially, I told him he was being ridiculious, that we wouldn't help him kill a man so he could slot straight into his shoes. When he told me it was the only way to get Hadley out alive, I stopped and listened. He wouldn't elaborate on that comment, making it clear that it's my girl's story to tell.

All he would say is that without our help, he and Hadley were in danger. That was enough to get me, and subsequently, my father and Hawke, on a chopper back to the mainland.

My father had already arranged transport with the Brooklyn office for upon our arrival, which seemed to upset Gerrick, but eventually, he shrugged it off and told us to follow him. At first, I had no idea where he was leading us, until we hit that familiar stretch of road that led to the one place I swore I would never walk in again—the hospital where Sherlyn died.

With nothing to go on, my mind started wandering.

I was thinking the worst, but could you blame me?

The last time we entered this place, we lost someone.

There were so many questions I wanted to ask, but the only one who could give me the answers I was seeking was driving in the car in front of us. I found it strange to see him with no security detail at all, but when you believe you are as invincible as Gerrick Alexandria does, I suppose you fear nothing.

After arriving at the hospital, we continued following Gerrick through the corridors. His refusal to speak to any of us unnerved me, but that didn't stop him from walking silently ahead.

Flashbacks of a year prior flashed through my memory like a lightning bolt, and I freaked as we approached one of the rooms.

For the fucking life of me, I could not move.

Unsure of whom he was leading us to, I was stuck in the doorway. My gut told me it was Hadley, which had every inch of my body frozen, rooted to the floor. Eventually, the comforting hand on my shoulder and whispered words in my ear by Hawke thawed my frozen demeanor, allowing me to enter the room.

Once inside, I realzed that all my panic had been for nothing, because sitting upright on that bed was my beautiful girl. Her smile as we entered lit up the room, and I quickly crossed the small space, engulfing her in the biggest embrace I could manage. There was no way I wanted to let her go, but I did finally, when she whispered in my ear that she was okay.

When I pulled back, Hadley's eyes found mine, and for just one moment, our sights were firmly fixed on each other. I swear I saw tears well in the corners of her eyes, but it was only momentarily.

Reaching up with her hand, she gently touches my cheek and blinks rapidly a couple of times. Instantly, that vulnerability that I had glimpsed is gone, and replacing it is a hardness I have never seen in her gaze before.

Turning toward her brother, she sighs quite loudly, and from the corner of my eye, I see the puzzled exchange of looks between my father and Hawke.

"You look like shit," she scolds Gerrick. "Are you using?"

I fucking knew it!

"Does it matter?" he replies.

With his gaze fixed firmly on the door, he refuses to look at his sister. It's as though he's waiting for someone to walk through it.

"Of course it fucking matters, Gerrick," my girl states harshly, her menacing scowl boring into him regardless of whether he's paying attention to her or not.

"You need to leave. Go home and clean yourself up."

Finally picking up on her angry tone, he turns his head in her direction. In the whole time he has been seated, his fingers have fidgeted. Nodding, he rises slowly and leaves the room.

"All right, let's speak," Hadley directs at my father once her brother has left the room.

"Do you believe it is wise sending him away like that?" my father queries.

We all stared in silence when he left without saying a word. It'd been like the three of us didn't exist.

"He was looking for a reason to leave," she sighed. "I just gave him what he wanted."

It's hard to question her reasoning, considering we know nothing of their relationship.

"What do you want from us, Hadley? Why are we here?"

My fathers tone is flat, but not harsh like I expected. What worries him is the danger it's putting me in. He made it clear on the plane that if the choice is me or Hadley, he wouldn't think twice about walking away. I understood that, and it's comforting to know how much he cares, but I don't think I could leave her behind if her life was in danger.

"I want out," she declares.

There's no indecisiveness in her voice; she is very clear about what she wants.

"Gerrick wants to take over, and I want away from this life and this family."

Glancing over at Hawke, he turns back to tell Hadley that he and Hawke need to speak. When they leave the room, I sit beside my girl and take her hand.

"I don't blame them if they choose to walk away, Sean," my girl quietly states. "I am a criminal, and I understand the predicament I'm placing you in by having you here. He just wants to protect you."

Looking into those beautiful brown eyes of hers, I see her torment. "I just wish my own father felt the same way about me."

With that, she looks over toward the door as my father returns. Her hand grips mine harder, and there's something I have never witnessed on her face before—*fear.*

"We will help you, Hadley, but only because my son loves you," my father proclaims as he stands beside me near her bed.

"There will be conditions you must agree to first."

I thought for sure he would walk away, especially after what happened to Sherlyn.

"And those conditions are?" Hadley inquires.

"You must walk away and stay away. If I find out that you're involving my son, or my family, in this lifestyle, I will place you behind bars myself."

"Done," she quickly replies.

"Another thing, we need information on some associates of your fathers. I believe you know them well."

What associates is he talking about?

Am I not privy to something here?

I read that file of Hadley's back to front a dozen times.

What am I missing?

"Is that all?" she replies promptly.

Yeah, I'm definitely missing something here, and I've no doubt my father knows more than he is letting on.

"Yes."

"This seems too easy. What's the catch?" I hear her ask.

"No catch. You walk away and whatever investigations against you disappear. It would be wise for you to accept my generosity and ask no further questions."

The harshness I was expecting earlier from my father has surfaced. He doesn't like being challenged, and Hadley is strong willed enough to push those boundaries.

"Okay," she agrees in defeat.

She should be happy. She's getting everything she wants without any repercussions for the crimes she has committed, yet she doesn't look happy at all.

Is it Gerrick?

He would be the only reason Hadley wouldn't want to leave Brooklyn.

"I'm going to leave you now, but I will be back later. We need to check in with head office."

Kissing her cheek, I pull away, only to find resistance. My girl's hand is firmly holding on to mine, not allowing me to move.

"I promise you, Hadley, I will return. We have guards at the door. Your father cannot get to you."

Nodding, she lets me go, but not before pulling me in for one final kiss.

"Please come back soon," she calls out as we walk out of her hospital room.

I promise that I'll be back as soon as I can and go wait beside Hawke as my father speaks to the agent keeping guard. We apparently have four of them hidden. The only visible one is Agent Waldock, who is stationed outside Hadley's door.

"Let's go, son. We have work to do," my father calls out after leaving instructions.

He will also want to speak with Gerrick as well.

HADLEY

I wish Sean didn't have to leave.

I hate being in this room alone.

It's got a creepy vibe to it.

I know there's someone guarding the door, but if my padre wanted to get to me, nothing would stop him. We have had doctors and nurses in this hospital on our payroll for years.

If my padre wants me dead, it will happen regardless of who is around. I saw the way they looked at me when Gerrick brought me in. At the time, though, I didn't realize they knew what my padre was doing. Now I'm too scared to sleep in case they sneak in during the night.

"Hadley?" a soft male voice asks near the entrance.

He's dressed in a white coat, so I'm assuming he's a doctor. I've never seen this one before. I wonder if he's new?

"Hadley?" he asks again.

"Uh, sorry, yeah that's me."

The fact that he's new had me distracted for a moment.

"Okay, good." He smiles. "I'm Dr. Roberts, and I was just coming in to tell you I'm releasing you in the morning."

Huh?

"Umm, what happened to Dr. Scott?"

"Off playing golf. He asked me to look after you," he answers happily.

I don't know what to make of this one. He's nothing like the usual doctors I deal with in this place. For one, he's a lot younger and a hell of a lot hotter than any of the others. Secondly, he has to be new because I've never seen him before.

"Lucky him," I reply, smiling back. "You're new, right?" I ask.

"What makes you think that?" he asks in return.

"I've never seen you around here before, and you're hotter than the regular doctors."

This time, I make him blush.

He's definitely young, much older than me, but still young.

"Yes, I'm new, I started a week ago, and thank you for the compliment. Now let's get back to me discharging you, or do you want to stay?" His cheery demeanor is hard to resist, and I find myself smiling along with him.

"Do you have someone who can pick you up? I'd rather you not leave alone," he questions before reaching my door.

"Yes."

I will message my *fratello* to come get me, but he'd better not be *fucking* high when he gets here. If he is, I'll be pissed.

"Oh good," he tells me, turning back around to leave my room.

Sending a message to Sean, I arrange for him and Gerrick to be here when I'm released in the morning. Although I'd love to have him here beside me now, I know he's better off by his padre's side. Allowing my tired eyes to win their battle, I finally close them so sleep can consume me.

"Hads," a gentle voice murmurs in my ear.

"You need to wake up, baby girl."

This time the voice is louder. Opening my eyes, I see Sean standing by my bed.

His face is pale. Something is wrong.

"Sean, what's wrong?"

Sitting up, he moves closer, engulfing my hand in his as he sits beside me.

"G-gerrick," his voice stammers.

"Gerrick what?" I demand.

"Gerrick has had an overdose. He is in the ER. We've just brought him in."

No. *Fucking*. Way!

This cannot be happening.

I don't know what to say.

"We found him in time, Hadley. He's alive."

I know Sean is talking to me, but I'm in shock. This has to be the work of my padre.

"I know this is a shock to you, baby girl, so I'm going to keep talking." Sean softly tells me.

It's like he can read me, that one. Sitting, holding on to his hand tightly, I listen as he continues.

"When we arrived at Gerrick's apartment, there was no answer. I tried his cell, but nothing. I could hear it through the door, but when no one picked up, I had Thomas kick the door in so that we could get inside."

That fratello of mine never goes anywhere without his cell, which for me would have been the first sign that something was wrong. Sean wouldn't have known that, though, and I'm grateful he took the initiative.

"We found him slumped on his bed with a needle hanging from his arm. He was barely breathing, Hads. We called for help and got him here as quickly as we could."

I feel for him, I really do.

This beautiful boy in front of me has seen more pain and death in the past couple of years than he ever should have for someone his age.

Fuck, Gerrick and I should've never seen the amount of death and pain that we have either. Gripping his hand as tightly as I can, I reassure him that it will be okay. Gerrick is strong; he will fight. It's not his first round in the ring.

My fratello and I are resilient. We've overcome so much over the years. and we will come out on top.

Our padre will not beat us.

"You ready, gorgeous?" my sweet boy's voice drifts into the small bathroom.

Now that I'm dressed and ready to leave, I'm nervous. My padre will be in Gerrick's room, and I don't know if I'm ready to face him. Sean comes up behind me, his arms circling around to sit on my stomach. I can feel his face buried in my hair, and it's calming. Relaxing into him, I close my eyes and take a deep breath.

"Ready when you are," I reply.

Gathering my stuff, we leave the room.

When we arrived at Gerrick's room, my padre wouldn't allow us to enter. His bulky frame blocked our view as he stood in the doorway. Edging my head left, I could only catch a glimpse of the doctors and nurses hovering over Gerrick.

"Go wait in the visitors area down the hall, Hadley. I will summon you once the doctor is finished. You know Gerrick wouldn't want you to see him like this."

That is such bullshit, and he knows it! And I'd love to yell it at him, but it won't do me any good. It certainly won't get into Gerrick's room any quicker, and my padre will only have me thrown out of the hospital.

I wonder if my madre is also down there waiting?

My padre's eyes reflect a hardness that matches his stolic face and rigid body. He looks like a statue, a hard obstacle that I won't be able to pass, with his arms crossed over his chest. Glaring at him in return, I turn to leave.

Always the asshole, he grunts, "And leave the trash where it belongs."

I want to stop and retaliate because I know he is talking about Sean, but a firm grip on my elbow stops me. Looking to my right, Sean just smiles at me and guestures for us to keep walking.

Obeying, I follow him, stewing on the the fact that if it wasn't for Sean, Gerrick would be dead right now. Unfortunately, the harsh reality is that Gerrick dying is what my padre would have wanted. Sean ruined his plans, and he will be wanting retribution. The knowledge that his figlia is involved only makes it messier for him. He will be more determined to eliminate us now before it affects his standing within the family.

My fratello and Sean were supposed to be the ones escorting me home, and yes, physically, I am healed and capable of being released today. Mentally, though, well, that's debatable, regardless of whether the doctor has given me the all clear to go home or not.

On our way toward the waiting area, Sean gives me more details about what they walked into at Gerrick's apartment. He said that once the other agent gained access, they proceeded to enter into darkness. He described it in a way that made it seem as if the silence was welcoming them.

When they found Gerrick, they initially thought he was passed out on the bed. So thinking he was asleep, they cautiously approached him. Once they saw the belt tied around his arm and the needle barely hanging from his skin, they called for assistance. When Sean finally saw his face, Gerrick's lips were blue.

Now I understand why Sean looked so visibly upset when he finally did reach me.

Sitting in the waiting area, it's no surprise that my madre is not here. I doubt my padre has even spoken to her. She will be none the wiser, but nothing about that is unusal.

Cuddling into my boy, I finally relax. We may be flanked by more CBI agents than I've ever seen before, yet I've never felt safer.

I should be worried that they will bring me in for questioning, except I'm not. Although he doesn't really know any details, Sean had whispered that all these men were here as our protection.

Apparently, Gerrick had told Sean and his padre that both of us were in danger, which meant that Sean's padre wasn't taking any chances. I'm still trying to work out if there is an ulterior motive behind his actions. In my experience, law enforcement don't do anything for nothing, and I have encountered more than my fair share.

A noise down the corridor catches my attention, and I look up just in time to see Jimmy, my padre's most trusted captain, approaching. Rising, I place my palm on Sean's shoulder to stop him from standing.

He can't come with me.

Sitting back down dejectedly, he glances up at me and only nods. I sigh in relief. It makes me happy to know that he understands that I can't put my fratello through any more trauma than he's already suffered.

"We will be waiting," Sean's padre states.

His voice echos behind me as I make my way toward Jimmy and my fratello. When we reach his room, I halt momentarily, preparing myself.

Part of me wants to cry hysterically, but my stubborness will never allow that to happen, especially not in front of my padre. There's another part of me, a deeper, darker side that wants to escape so that it can rip my padre to pieces, painting these perfectly white walls crimson with his blood.

Ignoring his presence, I walk toward to Gerrick.

His beautiful face as he sleeps looks peaceful, childlike almost, only it's ghostly white, with no color in it at all. Standing beside him, I pull his hand into mine as I always do, hoping he will wake and show me those eyes of his I love so much. I can't and won't lose him. Gerrick is the only true family I have.

"He's sleeping, Hadley. He's not dead."

Regardless of whether I want to or not, my gaze finds its way to my padre. The monster standing on the otherside of Gerrick's bed is the reason he is there, and if he believes he'll find a loving look in my eyes, or gratefulness, *he's very mistaken.*

I feel nothing but contempt for this man, the man who calls himself our padre.

"I'm not a child, Padre. I can see this for myself," I snipe in return.

"Watch your tongue, girl," he growls.

"Why? What will you do? You failed to silence me before, and Gerrick lying in this bed is no thanks to you."

"Are you insinuating something, child?" he growls. "I had nothing to do with this. Your fratello is in this bed because he overdosed."

Fucking Gerrick and his fucking drugs.

Closing my eyes tightly, I lower my head. I don't care what that bastard says. Gerrick is here because of him.

"Oh, you had something to do with this," I tell him tightly, opening my eyes again to glare back up at him. "What extent will you go to to get rid of us permanently?"

I have his full attention now.

"Are we that much of a threat to you?"

I would rather not do this over my fratello's sleeping form, but I don't think I'll ever get the opportunity again.

"What did you do to his supply?" I interrogate further. "It had to be part of one of your shipments. Gerrick knows better than to buy from your competition."

I can practically see the smoke billowing out of my padre's ears. He is seething.

There is a fire burning behind his eyes that is threatening to engulf me in his anger. If we were having this conversation in his office, I'd be dead. That trigger-happy fucker would have shot me point-blank range, right between the eyes.

How do I know this?

I know because I know my padre.

We are alike, and it's something I would have done, especially if someone had disrespected me the same way I just did to him.

"What you believe means nothing to me, Hadley. Your fratello lays in that bed becaue he is a junkie. A coke-sniffing whore who has outgrown his usefulness."

That may not have been a confession, but it does confirm my suspicions, and my padre knows it.

"Both of you have," he finishes.

I know I should ignore him, as he is just trying to get under my skin, but I can't.

"No, Padre, that's where you're wrong. It is you who has worn out your usefullness."

At that moment, Gerrick's grip on my hand tightens, but his eyes stay firmly closed. He is awake, but it's clear he doesn't want our padre knowing.

Playing along, I continue to torment him. "One day very soon, you and *Nonno* will be requainted."

Just when I think I see a fleeting moment of fear on his face, it changes.

"It won't be me, angelo, who will be joining your nonno. I have no intentions of giving up my seat just yet."

Turning to leave the room, he motions for Jimmy to follow, and just like the asshole he is, he leaves us with his parting words.

"Not without a fight."

Before I can reply, he's gone, Jimmy too.

SEAN

I wanted to resist, to tell Hadley I'd go with her to Gerrick's room.

Regardless of whether she wanted me there or not, I didn't like the idea of her going alone with one of her father's captains.

I knew I would've only upset her, so I just nodded and accepted that this was something she needed to do by herself. If there was any concern for her safety, my father would never have allowed her to go alone. All of us seated here know what Hadley Alexandria is capable of, thus the reason no one attempted to stop her.

There's a déjà vu feeling circling as I sit here waiting, and I don't know if it's because I'm still in shock from finding Gerrick, or if it's my memories of Sherlyn. I can imagine how daunting it would be for anyone who passes by, as there are about ten CBI agents, myself, my father, and Hawke.

That's a hell of a lot of testosterone in one small room.

Earlier, at Gerrick's apartment, I won't deny I was annoyed when I found him passed out on his bed.

Well I was, until I got closer to him anyway.

I've never seen a person overdose before, so imagine my shock when we found him lying on his bed with that needle in his arm. I'm no paramedic, nor have I ever had to perform CPR, so you can sympathize with me over my reaction to discovering that parts of him were already turning blue.

All I can say is, thank god Thomas was with me.

I didn't even have to say a word because by the time I'd turned to speak with him, he was already on his cell, calling for a medic.

Carefully removing the belt and needle from Gerrick's arm, I threw them to the side to check for a pulse. His lips were already blue, and I feared that we'd already lost him. Of all the stupid things he could've done, this way by far the worst, and I couldn't believe he'd fucking do that to his sister. She made no secret of her disapproval yesterday, so he obviously knew how much she hated him touching that stuff.

You'd think I'd be used to it now, the stuff I see, but it hasn't gotten any easier. I'm not even a goddamned agent yet. I'm just a wannabe—a kid who was dragged into this life willingly by his father. It all started as me being the computer nerd, the one who dug up shit on people no one else could. It's only been in the last twelve months that I've moved away from the screens and into the field.

The only fucking reason I was in Gerrick's apartment today was because of Hadley. She made me promise that I would bring him to the hospital. I know she's worried about her brother, but he's a no-good fucking junkie, a coke-snorting fucking criminal.

Well, that's what I believe he's using, anyway.

We'll know for sure when the results come back now that Hawke has organized the cleanup. After the medics took Gerrick, he sent in some of our guys to bag everything up. We are expecting the results on the tests Hawke ordered soon.

There was a lot of fucking powder in that kitchen for just one person, which makes us believe this was no random act.

Even my father agrees with that.

Both him and Hawke feel that Hadley's father has something to do with it, but once again, they are hiding shit from me. They are hiding the truth about what happened to Hadley that put her in hospital as well.

This is the kind of shit that they pull that eats at me inside The lack of trust in me is evident, and I'm growing tired of everything always being a need-to-know basis thing.

Distracted, I don't see my girl approach, I feel her touch instead. Her hand in my hair soothes where my thoughts are heading. Pulling her onto my lap, I cuddle into her, not caring who is in the room with us. Placing her head on my shoulder, she buries her face into my neck while twisting her arms around the back of me. Her warm breath on my neck turns me on, and my cock stirs.

The timing couldn't be any fucking worse.

"I can feel you, babe. Do you need help with that?" she teases, whispering in my ear.

I refrain from smiling or laughing when I catch sight of my father moving toward us from the other side of the room.

"How is your brother doing, Hadley?" my father inquires, stopping just in front of the two of us.

Standing, Hadley puts me in an awkward position, and she fucking knows it too. A sly grin in my direction before turning to face my father indicates that this litte vixen is enjoying my discomfort.

Refusing to move, I stay seated, my body hidden from my father, but not Hawke. Obviously catching on to my predicament, Hawke throws a jacket in my direction as discreetly as he can.

Another one with a sly smile, he just nods when I thank him before standing beside Hadley.

"He's okay. I spoke to him after my father left the room. He will be in for a few days but will make a full recovery," Hadley directs at my father and Hawke.

Using the jacket, I hide the fact that my cock is fucking harder than the uncomfortable plastic chair I've been sitting on for the past hour.

"We have also spoken about my father, and as much as I love his initative, we need to deal with this problem ourselves," she continues.

"This is not the time nor place for this discussion. We have men stationed here in the hospital that will watch Gerrick, but we need to move. This location is not safe for any of us," my father replies, his stern voice returning when business is put on the table.

"Lead the way," Hadley directs, motioning for my father to move.

GERRICK

I know I'm a screwup and that my life is fucked up. It's something I've been aware of for a long time, but what I don't need is Hadley reminding me. I love my sorella, sometimes more than myself, but fuck, she can be a righteous bitch when she wants to.

I've never been as strong as my sorella.

It's been pointed out on many the occasion over the years that I am the weaker of the two.

My padre and his crew have always made it clear exactly where I sit on the food chain, which is why I have worked so hard to prove myself over this last year. Only just recently, after Luca's attack, did I finally open up to Hadley and tell her about my drug use and what happened to me.

I'm good at hiding my pain.

I've always found it easy to fool people, except those closest to me, and regardless of what Hadley says to me or thinks, I did not set out to overdose.

I'm not heartless enough to ever put my sorella through that. She is the only family I actually give a shit about, and I know that it would kill her if anything ever happened to me.

When I left her hospital room yesterday, I was desperate.

It would've been obvious to everyone in Hadley's room yesterday that I was coming down off something. Seeing Hadley in that state and being in a room full of federal agents only made me more agitated than I already was.

I knew what I was about to do was wrong, and the moment I entered my padre's home, it became more apparent that I was making a huge mistake. The problem was, if I'd bought the coke off the streets or from one of our sellers, he would have suspected something.

When I walked through the door, it became obvious he was entertaining. He welcomed me, pulling me into his embrace to hug me against himself, but he was far too friendly. At the time, I thought nothing of it. My mind was on a mission, directing my body in one direction, toward my padre's stash of blow.

Cocaine and Hadley are my only weaknesses, and that fucking monster knew it.

Looking back, I should have been suspicious when I caught sight of those fuckers from Colombia. They were sitting in the living room talking to some half-dressed, drugged-up underage girls. Them being in Brooklyn had to be my padre's doing, but at the time, I didn't pick up on the suspiciousness of it.

By the time I walked through the door, my padre's party was in full swing. There were half-naked bodies strewn all over the place, with bottles of Jack Daniels and all kinds of drugs littering the tables. I must have looked like shit because I remember allowing my padre to lead me to the living room, where our Colombian friends were.

What's disturbing me right now is that it only comes to me in flashes. I can remember bits and pieces of the night, but nothing solid.

I'm not delusional.

I can see it for what it really was—a setup.

I should have recognized it straightaway, but I wasn't interested; all I cared about was forgetting.

I've seen some fucked-up shit since I started working for my padre, but the visions of Hadley tied to that desk by Luca were ones I struggled to erase.

When I arrived at the one place I should feel safe, I was strung out and in desperate need of a fix. My fucking padre knew I'd come crawling; apparently, I have become predictable.

Looking back now, there was nothing sponataneous or coincidental about what happened to me. My padre knew exactly what to expect, and he used it against me, arranging for Andres and Seb to be there.

It is obvious now that he contracted them to kill me.

When I awoke in that hospital room, I heard Hadley's and our padre's voices. There was nothing civil about their conversation. You could tell that sorella of mine was struggling to contain her temper when she was confronting him. Her voice was tight, and anger radiated through her words.

When I squeezed her hand, I felt her calm instantly.

I wanted to let her know I was awake, but I left my eyes closed to give her the hint that I didn't want our padre knowing. She played along, continuing to provoke him with her words.

I really have to get out of this bed before she gets to him.

If Hadley loses control, Padre dearest will be cut up into tiny little pieces. Her skills with a knife are beyond anything I've ever seen, but it's a dark place she slips into to become that person.

What worries me is that one day she will be lost completely, unable to find her way back out. Killing our padre will take her deeper into that darkness than she's ever been before.

He will not make it easy for her; his taunts will have a purpose. He wants her to break, to finally be that person he has been molding her into all these years.

He will have to kill me before I'll allow him to do that to her.

I can't let him succeed, not now that Hadley has a chance at escaping this family, and at happiness. This whole experience has definitely opened my eyes, and I won't be allowing anything like that to ever happen to me again.

I need to be stronger, if not for myself and the family, then for Hadley.

She wants out, and I will do everything in my power to make sure she gets what she wants. She deserves happiness more than I do. Unlike my sorella, I love this lifestyle.

What I need to rid myself of is the drugs.

Selling and distributing is one thing, snorting the *shit* is another, especially after it nearly cost me my life.

What started out as a headache while partying with Andres and Seb quickly turned into something I was in no way prepared for.

But then again, who does prepare themselves for an overdose?

I should have realized something was wrong, and I know I keep repeating that, but I'm not normally that stupid.

Maybe I was blinded, and it made me an easy target.

Andres and Seb were way too keen to take what I believed was our last hit. Andres had been overzealous with his hands, stroking my cock through my jeans. He was whispering in my ear what he was going to do to it with his tongue.

His touch and his words were putting me in a state of bliss that I was really getting into.

Fuck it, I thought.

All I wanted to do was relax.

The thing about those two is that they're familiar.

What Andres could do with his hands and mouth normally had me coming quicker than a champagne cork popping. It was just what I needed and so desperately wanted.

With both my arms placed firmly behind my head, I sank further into the comfort of the chair I was lounging on, with Andres and Seb on either side of me. My rock-solid cock was being roughly caressed by Andres, and Seb was whispering sexy words in my ear. I thought for sure I was going to fucking explode. I was that horny.

It was then that the anxiousness kicked in, and I could feel my body trembling slightly. I remember brushing it off, because I was high and trying to focus on what Seb and Andres were doing to my body.

Big fucking mistake!

I know now that it had to have been those two who spiked my supply and that my padre *ordered* it.

Flashes of memories from last night have been pouring back in, yet I'm having trouble piecing those fragments back together to form a more stable timeline.

More disturbingly, being told that I was found with a needle hanging out of my arm freaked me out as well.

I have never injected myself there.

Everyone who knows me well knows that's out of character for me. The simple fact that I don't have any track marks is enough to corroborate my story.

I'm more the conspicuous type when using and prefer the gaps between my toes. The last thing I ever wanted was for Hadley to discover I used at all, let alone consider me a junkie. Snorting "white ghost," a term for cocaine that Andres uses, has always been easier, but I didn't want to end up looking like all the other coke freaks. I can always tell what people are using just from the little mannerisms they develop after a while. Long-term use of cocaine causes a constant sniffling or runny nose, which is why I alternate and inject between my toes as well.

For me, coke has always been my drug of choice.

Well, it became my drug of choice.

In the beginning, when my padre whored me out, I needed it so that I could deal with what those men were forcing me to do.

Andres and Seb were the worst.

Those two assholes did things to my body the first time that physically took months to heal.

Mentally, though, well, I'm still working on that.

I can't honestly say for sure that I've always been bi-curious, or if I just grew to love it.

Over the last year, I've wondered if I would've wandered down the same path if given the choice. Hadley, on the other hand, has always enjoyed the company of both men and women. She owns her sexuality, always has, and I've always been jealous of her strength and courage.

Another thing I remember is being in bed with Seb while Andres stood by the foot of it, watching us, his hand firmly grasping his cock. He was stroking himself as he watched Seb sucking my cock. Those memories are vivid, but so is the memory of my head pounding like a freight train running through it. Come to think of it, my body was shaking uncontrollably as well.

Shit! I really need to get out of this hospital room.

I'm not safe in here.

It won't matter how many federal agents are guarding me, if my padre wants to try and kill me again, he will find a way. I have to get to him first and more importantly, before Hadley does.

Everyone knows it should be that sorella of mine who succeeds our padre, but she doesn't want it.

She wants out, a life away from the violence.

I don't blame her because she's trying to exorcise that evilness buried deep inside her.

Hadley is craving a normal life, and as much as I hate law enforcement, Sean is her ticket out of here. After everything our padre has forced her to do, if she can grab at that happiness, who am I to try and take it away from her?

Our padre, though, would rather see her dead. He will never allow her to disappear, especially after he got a glimpse of what Hadley was capable of years ago with Andres's fratello. He recognized the evilness, one similiar to his own, and has been trying to control her ever since.

That girl has never been controllable—until Sean Valentine.

As much as I hate to admit it, that boy is good for Hadley. I've never seen her as happy as what she is when he is around. He brings out the girl she should be, and I love that. There's no hardness behind her eyes, just laughter and love. I would sacifrice everything to see my sorella happy, which is why we need to take down our padre, and soon.

When she was here earlier, we spoke about what happened. Hadley was upset with me, and yes, she has every right to be, but in the end, she understood.

Will she be so understanding if she catches me using again?

Probably not, but that's something I'll face when the time comes.

Removing the cocaine from my life isn't going to be as easy as that sorella of mine thinks it will be, but for her and her only, I will do it. My plans are to take over and lead our family, but I can't do that if I'm a drug-fucked cocaine addict.

One problem at a time, though.

For now, we need to work out a way to eliminate our padre so that Hadley can escape, and I think I know just the way to do it.

HADLEY

"Don't do anything you will regret"—that's what Gerrick said to me as I was leaving his hospital room.

What's there to regret?

AFTER THE DUST SETTLES

Killing our padre benefits us both.

He can take over as head of the family, and I can escape to be with Sean.

He worries about my state of mind, but he shouldn't. I need that evil bitch I keep hidden to surface so that she can show our padre exactly what he created and how it's going to be his undoing.

I will be the one to end his life.

I'm the only one capable of it.

Gerrick acts tough, but he's far from it. As soon as our padre opens his mouth, my fratello will let him get into his head.

That won't happen to me.

Nothing that man can say or do will change how I feel about him and what I need to do.

For now, though, I'll bide my time until the timing is right.

With Andres and Seb gone, scurrying away like insects back to Colombia, and Luca dead, my padre is vunerable. What allies he thought he had within the family are fewer than he will be expecting, thus forcing him to reevaluate his position.

Pity for him, I know all his strategies.

Now if he were a smart man, which he obviously isn't, he would have killed me himself instead of letting Luca play with me. That's a move he will be regretting now, especially since I have him at a checkmate. He may have been a master of this game, but he should have held back a few vital moves. Showing your hand completely is foolish, but then again, I don't think he ever expected for Gerrick and I to turn on him.

"What are you thinking about, Hads?" a soft, caressing voice breaks through the night silence. "Why are you still awake?"

Ah, there's worry in his voice now.

"I'm sorry, Sean, my brain won't slow down. It's scheming," I offer in honesty.

There's no point lying to him now. He knows more about me than I'd like, but that's what happens when the feds keep tabs on you.

"What can I do to take your mind off the top ten ways to kill your father," he jokingly asks.

"Sex," I quickly reply. "The hard, rough, fuck-me-stupid kind. Make me forget the last few days."

Sitting up quickly, I feel his arms wrap around my front, his chest hard against my back. Leaning into him, I can feel the hesitation in his movement. Although his padre is aware of what happened to me, I have asked them not to tell Sean. I will tell him soon what has happened, and I don't just mean with Luca. He needs to know it all to understand my mind-set. My hidden truths will have to be told to show him that nothing my family can do to me affects me.

Well, not in the way any normal person would expect anyway.

"That's not something that will help you right now, baby girl. You've been through enough over the last couple of days. Just lay back and let me cuddle you. Let me offer you security, a safe place to rest."

If only it were that easy.

Turning to face him in the darkness, I lay my palm to his cheek. "I know you won't understand, but I don't need you pussyfooting around me, babe. I'm not like other girls. If I tell you that I want you to fuck me, then just shut up and fuck me."

Gripping my face with his hands, he roughly pulls me toward him. His breath is raggard as he replies, "As you wish, Hadley."

Without any further words, he crashes his lips to mine and hungrily devours my mouth.

His own mouth is hot, and his tongue forceful as it enters through my lips, looking for its partner. Denying him nothing, my own tongue seeks his out as his kiss engulfs me, taking away my breath.

Pulling away slightly, reluctantly breaking our contact, Sean rests his forehead against mine. His breathing is as erratic as my own, but he refuses to remove his hands from my face.

Panting, I close my eyes and savor the moment we have found ourselves in. I can't recall a time, prior to Sean coming into my life, where I have felt this at ease in another person's arms.

It's sad to say, but I don't believe I have ever felt this comfortable, not even in my own madre's company. In this small fragment of time, nothing and no one can come between us. Whatever bond we are forming is stronger than anything I have ever felt, and I need to protect it.

I need to protect us.

Frankly, everything I'm feeling right now scares the living fuck out of me.

This is so not like me at all.

I'm a cold, heartless bitch who has never cared for feelings before.

Sex was sex.

Male or female, it didn't matter.

If I wanted to relieve the stress and tension of working alongside my padre and the creeps he associated with, I fucked. There was nothing emotional about it. I wanted relief, so I always took what I wanted, regardless of who I was with—until Sean entered my life.

With him, I always want more, which is something I'm not familiar with.

I'm used to getting down and dirty, but the things this boy makes my body feel are alien to me. When he breathes those dirty words in my ear just as he's ready to orgasm, my whole face heats up. I've never blushed before in my life; never had anyone who was capable of making me do it. Yet his touches do me in. They reach a place deep inside of me, spreading tingles throughout my body. It's a feeling that unravels me as it travels from my core upward, making me crave him like nothing I've experienced before. I will do anything to make sure that feeling never dies and that nothing ever happens to him.

Maybe God is offering me redemption after all, in the form of Sean Valentine. Maybe I can be saved and am being offered a second chance at life and happiness.

Falling back onto the bed, I'm pulled on top of him. His arms squeeze tightly around me as his lips find mine once again. Those kisses of his are gripping hold of me, mesmerizing me while they pull me under his control.

I have no will to fight the feeling of losing myself completely to him.

It is way too strong.

I don't understand how one person can entangle themselves with another to the point of losing all self-control. It's as if I can feel his fingers wrapping themselves tightly around my heart, refusing to let go, and I like it.

"I can't get enough of you, Hadley," he breathes against my lips. "You're so goddamned sexy."

Fiercely, I crush my mouth back onto his to forcefully take control, only to have Sean pull back. Stunned, I sit up suddenly, trying to focus on his face in the darkness.

Why would he do that?

Does he not want me?

"If you want this to happen, Hads, it's on my terms, not yours," he quietly tells me. "Rough is not what you need right now, regardless of what you think, especially not tonight."

As if sensing my hestitation, he pulls me down beside him to continue, "I'm not one of your fuck toys, beautiful. You can't use me like that. I love you, Hadley Alexandria, and I plan to show you just how much, but my way."

Tears well in my eyes at the realization of his words. I don't know if I truly believed him the first time he told me, but I do now. Every defined detail echoing throughout his voice sends chills down my spine.

Maybe he is right.

"Just go with it, Hads. Relax and let's just feel our way through this. I know I don't have the experience you're used to, but there's nothing stopping me from learning."

His words relax me, soothing me as I sink back onto the pillow, lying on my back.

"I don't need experience, Sean Valentine. I just need you."

Without words, his fingers find their way to the strap of my singlet, sliding it over my shoulder to expose my skin. When he gently kisses just below my neck, I freak for a moment. Sensing my apprehension, Sean returns to using his fingers to explore my body. Their touch delicately moves in gentle circular motions, making their way to my hardened nipples protruding through the fabric.

"I love how hard these get, Hads. They remind me of little pebbles, pushing their way through the material, thrusting themselves forward until I notice them."

His soft, silky voice is so goddamned sexy as it whispers across my body.

I love the innocent way he describes every little detail on my body like he is discovering it all for the first time. A deep groan escapes his mouth as he becomes more adventurous. Closing my eyes, I relax, allowing him to do whatever he pleases.

His weight gently presses into me, leaning across to take my other nipple into his mouth. I can feel the wetness on my shirt as he sucks and pulls on each nipple alternately. The sensations his mouth is causing are amazing.

No one has ever taken the time before to explore my body like Sean is.

I've never orgasmed from anything like this before, but if he keeps it up—the sucking of my nipple into his mouth as he wraps his tongue around and around before releasing it—I just might.

The nerves he's taunting with his actions are sending shock waves, little lightning bolts straight down my body. There is a tingling in my lily, a reaction to his zeroed-in attention on my breasts, that has moans filtering out of my mouth, none of which are ladylike at all. It's a good thing we are staying in a hotel room away from his parents, or I'd be in trouble, because all my moans are doing is encouraging him.

"Do you want me to stop, Hads?" he groans against my shirt.

His hands have moved, ever so slowly creeping their way up my sides, pushing the material along with them. Stopping just beneath my breasts, he is waiting on a signal from me, something to give him a green light to continue.

I love the feel of his hands on my bare skin, and with shallow breaths, I tell him, "Don't you fucking dare."

Lifting himself into a sitting position, he yanks at my shirt, pulling it upward until I have to move slightly to help him remove it. Lying back down, I look up into his eyes. They are lust filled, and it's as though he's drinking me in, savoring the sight. Regardless of how dark this room is, there's no missing what he's feeling and what he wants to do.

Placing his hands back on my sides, he slides them along the edge of the material on my bra. Following the seam, he traces it up along the cup, skimming the tips of his fingers along my flesh.

Each gentle touch makes my body arch upward, searching for more of his touch. When they reach the straps, he continues to tease, gently sliding them off my shoulders down my arms.

Without removing it completely, he pulls the cups down, exposing my breasts to the coolness of the room.

In anticipation, my nipples harden again, and shock waves shoot through me. Pinching each bud between his finger and his thumb, he roughly rolls them, torturing me in a purely erotic way. My body arches upward, closer to him, and I can feel his hard cock digging into my *lily* through our clothes.

He has me drenching wet and hot for him.

His slow progression is pure torture.

"I could do this to you all night, beautiful. I love how your body reacts to my touch, but it's time to explore."

And just like that he moves off me, leaving coldness in his wake.

Wanting to watch his next move, I open my eyes just as he removes my shorts. For a brief moment, he's just staring at my body. His gaze excites me, so I sit up and remove my bra, leaving myself completely naked.

"Undress for me, Sean, slowly, so I can enjoy the view," my breathless voice mumbles.

He slowly moves off the bed, turning on the bedside lamp. Walking backward, he steps far enough away to give himself room. The fact that he is doing this surprises me, but I won't complain. With agonizingly slow movements, he removes his clothing piece by piece, throwing it beside him, keeping his gaze firmly fixed on mine.

I don't know how I deserved someone as beautiful inside and out as Sean, but I'm fucking grateful. He is gorgeous, and when he removes his boxers, that hard cock bounces up, grabbing my attention. I'm loving that he's doing this for me, really fucking loving it.

I shift my gaze back up to his, and there's some serious heat burning through his eyes. With determined steps, he strides back toward me, only stopping when he reaches the edge of the bed.

Ever so gently, he gestures for me to slide around so that my feet are resting against him. Lowering himself, he kneels in front of me, sucking in his breath when he's face level with my *lily*.

I know everything about what he's doing should frighten me, but I feel nothing but love and lust.

He has my body craving him like a crazy woman.

All I want is for him to bury his face between my legs and claim me as his. I want him to possess every inch of my body and own it. As if sensing my need, he moves closer. His breath on my skin ignites those tingles deep inside of me, setting them off like fireworks.

How have I never experienced this before?

Distracted, I'm not prepared for his tongue hitting that other little bud. The one hiding behind the walls of my *lily*.

When I jump, he stops, so I reassure him I'm fine, and he continues.

Every lick of his tongue along the folds adds fuel to the fire he started, but it's not until he sucks that tiny little ball of sensitivity into his mouth that I explode.

Fuck me, that was quick.

With heavy breathing, I clench at the bedding beneath me to calm myself, only Sean has other plans. Lapping at the juices escaping, he drinks me in, reminding me of a man dying of thirst. It's absolute bliss, and instead of subsiding, my orgasm lingers, slowly building again as two of Sean's fingers make their way inside my *lily*.

Why do I call it that, you ask?

Well, because that's what my madre called it when I was little.

It's the only innocent thing left in me and something I refuse to let go of.

There's a moment in time when my madre meant the world to me, when I was about seven years old. I loved our time together and could never understand why she didn't live with us. I remember vividly walking to my padre's office to see if I could go to the park with Gerrick and our nanny when I heard him and my madre yelling at each other.

It's the only time I can remember her ever raising her voice at him.

She wanted to take me and Gerrick away with her, but my padre told her no. He said that the only way I would ever live with her was if I was put to work in one of his brothels. I didn't enter, walking back to my room instead. At the time, I didn't understand what he meant, but I knew it was bad.

Later on, before she left, my madre told me to never let anyone ever touch my private parts—my *lily*, as she called it. She told me that when I was older, I would want men touching it. I promised her that I would never let anyone touch me there, only to have her tell me that when I was much older, I would understand.

Over the years, her advice was forgotten because my padre didn't let anyone touch me, well, not until I turned sixteen. That was the only time he ever tried to force anything on me. I promised to do unspeakable things to him if he ever tried again. Needless to say, he channeled that into creating a monster, one who would be an asset to his operation.

As Sean's fingers increase in speed and his mouth grips my nipple, so does the momentum of my release. Within minutes of the last one, he has me exploding all over again on his fingers.

Satisfied, he sits back on his heels, wiping the moisture of my release from his face. There's a grin that slowly spreads across his face, and I can't help but recipocate.

"You look happy with yourself," I tell him breathlessly.

"You better believe I am. I nearly came all over the carpet. You were that fucking sexy," his gruff voice replies. "I'm going to have you doing that again and again before the sun rises."

Well, fuck me, aren't we oozing with confidence tonight.

"What, no, I'll have you screaming my name as well," I tease.

My own smile broadens as a loud gutteral laugh leaves his lips.

"Well, seeing you've mentioned it…" He laughs.

I can't help but smile, and I love that he makes that happen naturally. Normally, my smiles are forced, a false impression of who I am to impress padre's "business" friends. There's nothing fake about the feelings Sean brings out in me. He has me believing that there is hope—hope that I can become a better person, one capable of living a normal life.

Crawling onto the bed over me, Sean positions himself between my legs.

"I wanted to go slow, Hads, but you have me that worked up I doubt I'd last. My cock is already leaking."

And that's my cue.

Before he can do anything, I'm on my stomach lying in front of him, with his cock inches from my face.

"How about I have you screaming my name first?" I taunt, just before I take his length into my mouth.

His whole body shudders at my touch, and it excites me more.

Glancing up at him, I slide my mouth off him and tease the tip with my tongue. His eyes cloud over, and then his head drops back. He places his hands on his hips, and his back arches just enough to thrust his cock back into my mouth. As I place my palms on his thighs, he groans in ecstasy. The noises are sexy, and I take him deeper until he is hitting the back of my throat.

"Oh my god, Hadley, that fucking mouth of yours is heaven," he moans, thrusting his cock back into my mouth.

Never before have I wanted to let anyone take control like I want Sean to right now.

I don't want to think.

Just for once, I need someone else to take over and set the pace.

The narcissist in me wants to tell him that I told him I'd have him screaming my name first, but the last thing I want to do is ruin the moment.

It can wait.

Right now, I'm enjoying watching the pleasure on his face while his cock fucks my throat.

As if sensing my submission, Sean grabs hold of my hair, tightly gripping onto it, yanking my head in a back-and-forth motion.

Slowly, he increases his pace.

It won't be long now before he lets go completely.

Keeping my eyes on him, I watch as the pleasure takes over, and he quickens his movements to finally find his release. Just as he lets go, he opens his eyes and stares straight into my own. Sitting up, I let his cock slide out of my mouth, and I swallow his release, wiping my mouth while holding his gaze.

I want him to see what he does to me.

"You have no idea what you do to me, do you?" Sean quietly asks, inching his way closer to me. "You're a need I can't live without. I'm never letting you go again."

His words hit me deep. That heavy weight I've been carrying around all these years is finally starting to lift.

With Sean, I know I can rid myself of it for good.

"You'll tire of me one day, Sean. We are young. There's no guarantee you will always feel like this," I reply.

Just for a brief moment, my fear rears its ugly head, trying to put a damper on what should be a blissful moment.

"Never, Hadley. You're an addiction I can't fight. You are in my every waking thought when we were apart, and I need you in my life. That won't ever change," he reassures me.

Pulling me closer, he presses my body to his and just holds me. With his arms wrapped around my body, he does nothing more than comfort me.

"I don't know how to be mushy, Sean, but it feels like I can't breathe when we are apart, and I don't like that feeling," I confess. "I'll ride alongside you on this rollercoaster for as long as you'll have me."

Without releasing me, he kisses my forehead, pulling back slightly to look me in the eye as he tells me, "I'll happily take that seat beside you, beautiful girl. I'll never let anyone take you away from me again."

"Love me," I breathe.

And he does.

GERRICK

Waking with a start, I sense a presence, but it's too dark to see anyone. Twisting my head from side to side, I fight to adjust my vision.

A sickening feeling in my stomach tells me I'm not alone.

"Stop looking for me, boy," the voice in the dark says.

Instant recognition of the voice relaxes me slightly, if that's even possible. Glancing in the direction of the voice, my vision finally adjusts to the blackness, and I see my padre moving toward me.

Fuck. He's the last person I want to see right now, and how the hell did he get past those agents?

"Relax, Gerrick, I'm not here to kill you. And before you ask, I didn't do anything to the guard at your door. I had the nurse give him a sedative. He'll be asleep for a while. I'm here because I have an offer for you. A way to redeem yourself," he addresses.

There is nothing he could offer me that I would accept, and I'm not looking for his redemption. I want to take his place to be rid of him once and for all.

"I would rather die than take anything you have to offer," I hiss in return.

He's quiet for a moment, but his response is one I expected.

"That can be arranged, figlia," he snarls. "But I don't want to resort to that. I need you, Gerrick, I need you to take Luca's place by my side. The family needs you."

Playing along, I agree to listen to his proposal. I already know what he wants. He will want me to execute the hit on Hadley. That's the only way he will let me live. To prove my loyalty and earn redemption, I need to take my sorella's life. She's the one person I trust and love, and he fucking knows it too.

It's why he is here.

"Your sorella has become a liability, Gerrick. She can't be allowed to live. Her and the agent she's whoring herself out to," he declares.

Fuck, I didn't see that coming. I knew he would want me to eliminate my sorella, but not Sean.

"And if I say no?" I ask in return.

"Then you won't leave this hospital alive. If you think those agents can keep you safe, you're mistaken," his harsh voice replies.

I need to get out of here before it comes to that.

There's no way I'm taking the life of Hadley, but for now, I agree to appease him. When he gives me that god awful grin of his before he turns to leave, I know he's bought it. He actually believes I will carry out the hit on Hadley and Sean.

For now, though, I have to use that to my advantage and make my getaway before he realizes I'm lying to him.

There's only one place I feel safe.

I need to contact Hadley.

SEAN

My god, this water is hot, like fucking scorching.

Now that Hadley has gone to answer her cell, I've turned the heat up. She's been expecting a call from Gerrick, so there was no way she was going to let it ring out. His timing couldn't have been worse. It was right at that moment when I had my girl pinned to the shower wall, with her legs wrapped around my waist and my cock buried deep inside her.

When the ringing started, she freaked and left me standing in this shower on my own. I was so close too, just a few minutes later and she would have been filled with my cum. Instead, she left me to finish on my own.

I can't blame her, though.

Gerrick is the only family member Hadley cares about, and she's extremely protective of him. I don't know how either of them will cope when she finally leaves Brooklyn.

When I woke during the night and found her awake, I was concerned. It worried me, especially since she still hasn't spoken about the reason she was hospitalized. All I know is that it had something to do with her father's captain, the guy Gerrick killed.

I doubt I'm going to like it, but at least I know he's dead and can't hurt her anymore.

Not that I would allow anything to happen to her anyway.

I can't deny how much I wanted her.

I have since the hospital waiting room.

Her ass grinding on my lap had me so fucking hard, but then she went and left me high and dry. It wasn't hard to miss, and I was fucking humiliated. I thought for sure my father was going to notice, but Hawke saved my ass. The last thing I wanted was a lecture from him, and my girl just found it amusing.

All I wanted to do when I found her awake was to comfort her. A part of me wanted to bury itself inside of her warmth, but I assumed she would need time before letting me touch her. I was willing to wait as long as it took, yet when she told me to fuck her, I nearly came right there and then. I had so many thoughts running through my head, but the lust took over, and I kissed the life out of her, like I've never done before.

When Hadley put her mouth on my cock, I thought I was going to explode.

I was not expecting that.

What gripped me by the balls was her allowing me full control. It had me acting in a way I never have before, something like the whole alpha male shit my sister Sophie talks about. I ended up steadying myself and found myself in awe of the way Hads let me take over.

Getting our first orgasm out of the way paved the way for us to spend the next couple of hours exploring each other, although I also managed to bury myself deep inside of her as often as possible.

I fell in love with the way she came undone beneath me.

Her pussy gripped my cock so fucking hard that my body convulsed everytime she did it. She milked me dry every fucking time. Once I entered that sweet body of hers, I lost all control of my actions. I could have sworn my cock had a mind of its own and dictated my every move. By the time we had finished, I was spent, collapsing beside my girl and falling asleep instantly.

Shit, I'm hard again, but there's no time to deal with that now.

I need to find out what's going on.

"What the fuck, Gerrick!" I hear Hadley yell as I step out of the bathroom. "We are coming to get you. You're not safe."

Well, that doesn't sound good.

"Meet where?" she grunts in disapproval. "Make sure you are there, Gerrick. We will be there in an hour."

And with that, she hangs up.

Sensing that I'm there, she turns, her face grim.

"What's wrong, Hads?" I ask to break the silence.

"My father visited Gerrick last night. He's given my brother an out. If he kills both you and me, he'll take Luca's place by his side," she emotionally confesses.

There's a look of sadness shadowing her pretty face, but she should have anticipated this move. Her father was never going to give up without a fight. He will be using Gerrick's current state of mind to try and sway him.

Regardless of whether he goes through with the hit or not, he's dead. There's no way Jason Alexandria is going to make good on his offer. He wants his children dead, and he's manipulative enough to work every angle he can.

"I'm guessing Gerrick is disappearing," I finally reply.

Nodding, Hadley continues, "There's a place Gerrick and I would hide when we were kids, when my brother needed to escape his monsters. No one but the two of us knows the location. It's the only place he feels safe and where he knows they can't get to him."

After agreeing to help and dressing, we leave to find my father and Hawke. Both men are in my father's suite in deep discussion. As we enter, their eyes turn to us and their conversation ends.

Knowing that we have interupted, I'm cautious as Hadley relays what Gerrick has told her. Their first suggestion is to place him into federal protection, but she refuses. She tells them that there is only one place her brother will be safe, and he is already there. If we tried to move him, her father would find him and kill him.

When my father asked Hadley what she thought we should do, she told him that just she and I would go to her brother.

Over his dead body, he boomed at her.

He made it very clear that he wouldn't allow his son to come into harm's way.

She understood that, telling him that she would go alone.

It would be safer for everyone anyway.

She knows how to get in and out without being detected. The last thing she wanted to do was spook Gerrick any more than he already was.

I objected, but she paid no attention, telling me to trust her.

That's the thing, I do trust her.

It's Gerrick and her father who I don't trust.

Kissing my lips, Hadley leaves my father's hotel room, promising to return as quickly as possible. It's the look in her eye as she turns that final time that worries me. It's as though she knows there is trouble ahead but is protecting me, *keeping me safe*.

HADLEY

Leaving Sean behind was hard.

The concern that was written all over his beautiful face warmed my heart, but there are just some things that this girl needs to do herself. One day, he will accept I'm not like other girls, that I am more than capable of taking care of myself.

On the corner of Tenth Avenue and Prospect, there's an apartment complex. It's a run-down red brick building in a part of Brooklyn our padre never visits.

It's also home to a kind old woman who used to let us hide in her basement and feed us milk and cookies.

Renita is her name, and she used to fuss over us like we were her own children. Gerrick loves her, and we both make sure she never wants for anything.

There is no other place he would have felt safe.

When I approach the building on foot, something seems off.

This street should be busier.

There is a niggling feeling in the pit of my stomach that something is very wrong with this picture, and I don't like it at all.

Slipping through the gate behind the apartment, I notice Renita's car is missing. I'm praying that she is at work right now and not at home. Scoping out my surroundings, I realize it's way too quiet for this time of the morning. By my calculations, there should be more people out on the sidewalk by now, yet there is only half of what I'm used of seeing on any normal day.

Gerrick's in trouble.

Fuck.

I have to get into that building, *and fast.*

How the *fuck* did they know where he was?

We've never told anyone about this building. It's always been the one place we could escape to when bad shit happened. So you can imagine we came here often as children, until the day I learnt to fight back.

What the fuck happened?

Using some old pallets, I maneuver myself over an old brick structure and make my way round to the front. The only background noise that stands out is the parrot squawking in its cage over at the hardware place on the opposite corner.

A cool breeze suddenly flows past me, sending chills throughout my body.

Shivering, I get the sudden feeling of eyes on me. The thought freaks me out slightly as I enter through Renita's front gate.

Looking around, they could be hiding anywhere.

There are two-story buildings on every corner of the intersection. The openess of this particular suburb was one of the things we loved about hiding here. There was no chance anyone could sneak up on us because we would see them coming.

Raising my hand to knock, I notice that the door is already ajar. I don't know how my padre found Gerrick, but he's here, and they will be waiting for me.

I'm thankful I made Sean wait with his padre because this is a setup.

Our padre was obviously anticipating that Gerrick would run, and he would've had one of his goons following him.

That's the only way they would know about this place.

My fratello was wrong.

Our padre didn't believe him when he said he'd carry out the hit on me and Sean. That bastard set Gerrick up knowing he would take off and warn me. If this is the case, then he would have also known that Gerrick and I would arrange to meet.

We took the bait, and I only hope that my fratello is still alive.

Pushing the front door open, I enter cautiously.

After Luca blindsided me, I swore I'd never go anywhere unprotected again. Reaching behind, I free my knife from under my shirt and creep further into the room.

Not surprisingly, I find no one at all.

If they are anywhere, it'll be the basement.

Standard procedure for my padre will be to have another couple of men hiding, just in case something goes wrong. A quick sweep through the apartment highlights a few areas where his men could be, but it's nothing I can't take care of if a problem arises.

Moving back toward the stairs, I follow them down, hesitating momentarily when I grasp the handle that will lead me into Renita's basement. There's a mixture of fear and anxiety swirling in my stomach, caused by the fact that there's no noise at all coming from the room.

Just the thought of what our padre could be doing to Gerrick has my blood boiling.

Twisting the handle slowly, I push the door open and freeze.

Leaning, with his back against the wall, is my padre, in front of him, strapped to a chair, *Gerrick*.

His head may be slumped, and he is unconcious, but I can see the blood that's running down his cheek from a cut above his eyebrow. I'm paying no attention to the man who fathered us as he strides across the small space toward me, just my fratello.

"Come any closer, Padre, and I will gut you," I threaten.

My knife is resting by my side, but my hand is gripping it in readiness to attack. With my vision still directed at my fratello, I can't help but notice that my words momentarily stop my padre.

He's hesitant, and I don't blame him.

If Gerrick is dead, I promise I will splay his insides over the walls of this tiny basement.

The uncomfortable silence is deafening, but I refuse to budge.

Out of the corner of my eye, I can see my padre's *soldati* carelfully taking up position on either side of me. They are close enough to enable me to feel their presence, but not close enough for me to attack them. They are waiting on a signal from my padre.

"Now, now, angelo," he starts. "You of all people know that I was never going to just let you go. Everyone knows what I do to those who betray me, and you, my angelo, have betrayed me in a way I never imagined."

There's emotion in his words, which, although I have no care for, I also wasn't expecting.

When will he understand he can't guilt me anymore?

I'm not that naive or vulnerable.

The sixteen-year-old girl he sent to negotiate with his Colombian clients might have been, but she wasn't by the time she came home.

"Let me out, Hadley," the evil bitch inside of me calls, a voice that I don't need clouding my judgement right now.

"Pleeease let me out," she whines. *"I want to play."*

"I've no interest in what you do," I reply with a flat voice. "I stopped caring for you a long time ago, Padre. You've been dead to me since you tried to turn me into a whore."

I'm trying to focus on the monster standing in front of me, but that inner voice keeps whining like a two-year-old. She wants out, so that she can show our padre exactly who she is and what she is capable of.

I can't let that happen.

If she escapes, I'm scared that I'll lose who I am, and any hope of escaping will become a distant memory.

"To be honest, Hadley, that's all I thought you'd ever amount to," my poor excuse for a padre confesses. "A common whore like your madre."

No surprise there.

"Gerrick was supposed to be the one to take my place one day, the one groomed to succeed me."

Once again, no surprise.

"But after what you did to Maitas, I saw a potential in you I never did in your fratello."

Walking back toward Gerrick, he continues, "Gerrick is weak," he says, pulling on my brother's hair to lift his head so that I can see what has been done to him. "And nothing like you, my sweet child."

All I can do is glare at him.

"It was back when you murdered that man in cold blood that I knew who I had to groom as my sucessor. With those roles now reversed, Gerrick only became of use to me as a whore."

Shifting my vision to look into my padre's eyes, I find nothing but blackness—a darkness much like that of a man with no soul.

Gripping Gerrick's hair harder, he forcefully yanks his head to the side.

In the short amount of time I have spent around Sean and his padre, I couldn't help but notice how close they are. There's an unbreakable bond between the two of them and a protectiveness I'm not familiar with. When I told them that Sean and I would come to Gerrick's rescue, Sean's padre went all caveman on me. If the situation I found myself in wasn't serious, I would have laughed.

Never in my whole life have I seen my padre react in such a manner toward me or Gerrick. We have never been anything more than pawns in a very strategic chess game, a game where loyalty and trust are easily dissolved, depending on how bankable your skills were to him.

"You know I plan to do the very same to you, right?" I sneer, my lips curling into a smile. "By the time I finish, I will have painted the walls red with your blood, Padre dearest."

His eyes widen, and shock registers on his face.

This amuses me.

Me smiling at him has obviously thrown him off, but don't be fooled, it won't last for long.

There's a churning in my stomach, a sickness that swirls in twists and turns, trying to escape upward throughout my body. It's evil, and if it escapes, no one is safe. Finding his resolve, his face hardens, and he sneers back at me.

"There are three of us in this room with you, *angelo*, and two more upstairs. Even if you could do harm to one or two of us, you wouldn't make it out alive."

"You underestimate what I'm capable of," I quickly throw back at him, moving slowly toward Gerrick.

Taking a hesitant step, he moves backward, closer to the wall. I know he's scared of me; his fear is written all over his face. It doesn't matter how much he tries to hide it, he's terrified of what I'm capable of doing to him.

He should be scared.

He created this, *and me.*

Behind me, his goons edge closer, just in case. I know that if I tried to lunge at him, they would get to me first. I'm not stupid, I know I'm not invincible. There's no way I can overpower all three.

I will have to be smart about this.

Kneeling in front of my fratello, the track marks in the crease of his arm look fresh. Whatever they have given him was only recent, but it was enough to knock him out.

Checking his pulse, I make sure he is still alive.

Gerrick is all I have in this fucked-up world.

Well, he was, until I met Sean, and I won't lose him, especially not when we are this close to ridding the earth of our scum of a padre.

Satisfied that he is okay, I rise back to my feet, turning to see how close my enemy is.

"I have an offer for you, Hadley," my padre's voice echoes.

My head snaps back around.

"Get rid of the agents, figlio, and come back to me, and you and your fratello can walk out of this room alive."

He's fucking dreaming if he thinks I'm doing that.

"If I refuse?" I reply.

"Then I will succeed in killing you both. Your precious feds can't help you this time," he confidently declares.

Seems as if he has found some confidence after all.

"I don't answer to you anymore, and you no longer have the power to intimidate me," I declare in return. "Regardless of my answer, I know you better than that. You have no intention of letting us leave."

"*Pleaseee, Hadley, let me out*," my evilness calls through the silence.

I'm so tired of all the fighting.

Maybe I should just let her out, so she can show them what she is capable of doing.

"There's no fooling you, girl. I should've known you wouldn't fall for it."

An admission, *finally*!

"I just needed to get you here, and Gerrick was the perfect bait."

More truths.

"I don't trust either of you anymore, figlia. You and your fratello are liabilities now, ones that I am forced to deal with."

Moving back to us, he stops just short. There's still a glimpse of fear reflecting in his eyes, but he's desperately trying to radiate confidence. He knows that if he gives me anything to work with, he will be dead.

Regardless of what he thinks, I will kill him.

I just need the right moment to strike.

I also need to work out what I am going to do about the two thugs who have inched their way even closer to us. All three of them are attempting to crowd around us in an attempt to frighten me.

I should be terrified, but I'm not.

"*You know you want to, Hadley*," that annoying little bitch chants. "*You know you want me to kill him*."

"Slide your knife over here, child. You won't be needing it," my padre orders, his voice gaining in strength with each word that spews from his mouth.

Doing as he asks, I slide the blade toward him, praying that he doesn't notice that it's not my favorite.

I'm not stupid.

I never go into a fight with just one weapon, but thankfully, Padre doesn't know that.

"Good girl," he praises.

There's a sickening grin now lining his mouth, all because he thinks I'm weaponless. He's under the false impression that he's safe and in control, but little does he know my favorite blade is resting against my leg, easily accessible.

I shoved it into my boot when I was getting dressed.

Still in a squatting position, I pretend to be looking at Gerrick. The handle of my blade sticks out just over the top of my boot, making it easy for me to grip it. The goons behind me keep edging closer and closer, but my focus stays on my padre who is also making his way back toward me.

Bending, he picks up the knife.

His eyes never leave mine, giving me his unwavering attention, but no matter how much he rambles, there's always going to be that element of fear everytime he approaches me.

It's there in his eyes, that flicker of doubt—my signal to strike.

Just as I attempt to grab hold of the handle, there are hands grasping onto my shoulders, pulling me upright. Twiddle Dumb and Twiddle Dee grip my arms, holding me still. Patience is going to be the key to overpowering these three, so just for now, I will allow them to hold me still.

Narrowing my eyes, I watch while my padre comes to a stop in front of me. Lifting the same blade I surrendered, he starts ranting about what a disappointment it has been for him to have not just one but both of his children turn against him. He rambles that he and I were more alike than he had ever imagined, and it gave him hope that if anything happened to him, the family would have a strong, confident leader.

"Pity it has to be this way, Hadley," he tells me. "We've never profited as extravagantly as we did when you were with us. You have a head for business, my girl, and up until now, you've let me capitalize on it. When did I start losing you?"

My mouth opens to reply, but he refuses me the opportunity.

Turning his back on me, he continues to ramble about it being Sean's fault.

He believes that if Vincent hadn't chased after that girl, we would've never attracted the attention of the Valentines. Little does he know, we've been on their radar for as long as we have had the feds harrassing us. This all started with Silo, and as much as I loved that man like a padre, it is because of him that we find ourselves utimately in this position.

When Gerrick twitches, I immediately glance his way. I can only hope that the goons securing me also don't notice.

He is waking.

Maybe there is a chance we can do this after all.

"I should have sent Luca to kill that brat that day," I hear my padre say.

I was so completely focused on my fratello that I had stopped listening to him.

"But no, he believed you wouldn't have any problem disposing of him. Against my better judgment, I allowed it, and look where it has gotten me."

"Hadley, it's time you let me free. We can end this now."

She's not giving up.

Her voice echoes in my brain, begging me to let her out.

Maybe I should. If I have any hope of escaping, it'll be with her egging me on.

Interrupting my padre, I tell him, "You're rambling, old man, and it's boring me. There isn't anything you can say that's going to impact my decision to kill you."

AFTER THE DUST SETTLES

His face pales, making me smile, "You're only delaying the inevitable by having your goons restrain me. That monster you created," I taunt, "she's calling to me, begging me to set her free."

His gasp is unmistakable. "She has plans for you, Padre, plans of showing you what she can do—what you have molded her into."

"Move her over toward the wall," he yells.

His screech startles both the idiots holding on to me, but they quickly shuffle me behind Gerrick toward the wall my padre was favoring earlier. The only good thing about the situation I find myself in is that if my fratello is waking and no one is noticing.

I'm going to need his help to take down our captors inside this room before we tackle the two upstairs.

"You want to play games, is that it?" he queries.

There's still that element of fear in his voice.

Does he not understand that I can hear it, that it's fueling me?

It doesn't matter how tough he attempts to act in front of his men. He can't hide that underlying fear that I cause. My smile only gets bigger at his words.

I'm past being scared.

I'm in survival mode now, and it's him that should be terrified.

"You think this is funny, Hadley?" he continues to query.

"More than you can imagine," I finally reply.

"You don't scare me, Padre dearest. The hold you had on me ended long ago. Everything I've done since that night I tortured and slayed Maitas has been of my own free will."

The laugh that escapes his mouth is a haunting one. For some reason, he still thinks he holds the upperhand.

Time to test my theory.

Before I left Gerrick's side in the hospital, he told me that he had the backing of our padre's soldiers. They had assured him that if he ever challenged for top spot they would support him.

Now it's time to determine who the two holding me down are really loyal to.

"Tell me, Padre. Why is there only four men here with you today?"

His heads snaps toward me instantly, an angry scrowl over-taking his face.

"Because that's all I needed to overpower the two of you," he spits in return.

Now for the fun to begin.

"My turn," a sinister voice inside whispers.

"Let's challenge that theory," my inner evil declares.

The stunned look on my padre's face gives away the fact that he's realized something is not quite right with me. He's right in his observation, and it's about to get a whole lot worse for him.

"You look like you've seen a ghost, Jason," she taunts.

The use of his name throws him off, especially since I've never called him that—ever.

Taking a step back, he just stares at me.

All I can do is watch from afar.

It's as though I'm here but I'm not.

My control over her gone for now.

Regaining his composure, he steps forward once more. "Since when do you call me by my name, Hadley?"

"I'm not Hadley. I'm Nereza," she replies in a voice much deeper and huskier than my own.

From where I am hidden, I watch as his step falters. There's a look of shock on his face, his features wincing in pain.

What the fuck.

"What the hell is going on here?" he asks, his voice shaky. "Where did you get that name from?"

"What's wrong, Jason? You look like you've seen a ghost." This Nereza continues to taunt.

"Release me and help Gerrick," she demands of the two holding us still.

Without hesitation, they let go and go to Gerrick's side.

"What the *fuck* are the two of you doing?" my padre bellows.

"Whatever I tell them to do," my fratello's voice echos through the darkness.

Considering it's midmorning, there's only random streams of light filtering through the windows into the room. It gives the appearance that it's nighttime, which under normal circumstances, makes these kinds of interrogations much more intimidating.

"You see, Padre, it's you who has been set up," Gerrick speaks once more.

"The faith in your ability to lead our family has diminished, and I'm challenging you. As soon as I set that in motion, your loyal soldiers deserted you, choosing to move forward with someone younger and smarter."

I've got the best seat in the house, front row. I may not have complete control, but I'm still able to witness everything as it happens.

"Restrain him," Gerrick demands of Twiddle Dum and Twiddle Dee.

Without hesitation, they move toward my padre, grabbing hold to pull him down onto the very chair my fratello had just occupied. I find it funny because all this was done with more resistance than I have ever seen my padre put up. He's thrashing his body around, trying to break free of the two large men's hold. All his fighting for freedom is useless because quick work is made of tying him to the chair.

Stepping back, Gerrick whispers something to them both, and they disappear up the stairs.

There are a lot of curse words spewing from my padre's mouth, but at least he's given up trying to get free.

It's hard to explain where I have gone, or what my brain has created to allow that deep dark evil to escape. It's as though I've stepped through a mirror and am watching from the other side. I can hear and see everything that is going on around me, yet I'm powerless to do anything. All I can do is watch as my padre continues to shout at us both, yelling obscenities that he thinks will help his cause.

"No point in speaking, Padre," Gerrick tells him. "You've done the one thing I have been trying to avoid."

This grabs our padre's attention.

"The evilness you've released from inside your figlia has no concious. She's as Nonna would describe it—a soulless being who lacks the ability to feel."

A hideous laugh escapes my throat, and all I can do is watch as Nereza uses my body to walk around my padre in circles. The blade I had secured is now twirling in my hand, as though she's using it to threaten. As we continue our path around the chair, Gerrick continues talking from his place at the foot of the stairs.

"You see, the girl circling you feels nothing except the thirst for blood."

As my body comes full circle, through this mirror, I'm watching as padre's eyes bulge. He is finally aware what is happening and how he no longer has any control at all.

"Make no mistake," my fratello explains. "The only way this is going to end is when Nereza here satisfies her taste. Only then will my precious Hadley be allowed to return."

What does he mean, "only then"?

Has he seen this happen to me before?

Why don't I remember?

"Do what you will. I have made my peace," an exasperated man sighs.

The realization that he will not escape has finally set in, but the question burning my lips is, how do I escape this room when Nereza has finished what she is here to do?

"Relax, Hadley, I've got you," her voice filters through my brain.

What am I thinking?

Of course she knows my thoughts.

We are one person, split by our demons.

"Do you understand yet, Padre?" Gerrick asks of him. "Do you finally see what you have created?"

A resigned figure looks up at us both.

Yes, at both, as I now find myself right beside my fratello, looking down at a defeated man.

"Your figlia has a split personality. You came here today to break, Hadley, but she has been broken for years. She's just good at hiding it, from you, from me—*shit*, from everyone."

No, that can't be true.

"I didn't create…this thing standing in front of me. She did that all by herself," he spits out hoarsely.

Sitting himself up straight, he prepares himself for the final confrontation. It won't be much longer before my fratello walks away and leaves the other me to finish our padre off.

"Regardless of the lies your madre told you, your births were no accident. I needed an heir, a figlia to take over my throne when I could no longer lead. When Hadley was born, I told your madre to give me one more child. If that child turned out to be another girl, then I would find someone who could give me a boy."

165

His admission explains so much. If I had control of my body, I would have slumped down onto the bottom step in shock because shocked is what I am.

"Don't falter now, girl. He is trying to get to you. Ignore his words. Ignore him," my alter ego comforts.

She is right.

This is his last-ditch attempt to hurt us.

"I had no need for a girl," Padre admits.

"Women are only useful for one thing—sex. They aren't leaders, and then your sorella here went out and proved that theory wrong. What she did to Maitas—"

"You mean what I did to Maitas," Nereza confides, cutting Padre off.

"You sent Hadley to die. She was never supposed to survive. But she did, and that was the night I came into existence."

Circling once more, I can do no more than watch as the blade slices through Padre's skin with each step I take.

"She was screaming in her head for help, for someone to save her from the agony Maitas was inflicting on her. So much pain. I could hear her and soothed her fears with reassuring words that I would help."

The fear on Padre's face has escalated. He is terrified and crying out in pain as the blade pierces his skin over and over again.

"I waited until that fat bastard had finished and then whispered to our girl to let me take over. She was beyond exhausted and gladly handed over the reins. I won't bore you with details, because you are well aware of what happened that night, and that he got what he deserved."

Glancing sideways, Gerrick has made himself at home on the bottom step, watching, observing only. He is letting Nereza run the show, gladly taking a backseat.

"Do you know the only time when Hadley wouldn't let me help her?" she asks Padre, the blade now positioned under his chin, pushing into his Adam's apple.

"No," his shaky voice replies.

Gulping loudly, there are tears streaming down his cheeks that I never noticed before.

"Don't let them fool you," Nereza whispers.

"When Luca attacked her. I tried to get free, but Hadley wouldn't let me. It didn't matter how hard I tried. She wouldn't let me out to gut that asshole. Just like I did to Maitas."

Maybe I can control her.

"I have business to attend to," Gerricks voice bursts through the room. "I'll leave the girls to take care of you, but, Nereza," he directs at me, "when the job is done, I want my sorella back. Are we clear?" his forceful voice asks.

"Yes," Nereza replies before turning back to padre.

"Good," he states before removing himself from the room.

SEAN

My nerves are on high alert as I stand and wait at the top of these stairs. When Gerrick called earlier, he was just leaving his hospital room. He had organized for some of the men loyal to him to let slip that they knew where Gerrick may be hiding.

He wanted his father to find him.

He wanted to trap him.

I was worried because his voice sounded panicked, and his concern for his sister was obvious. More to the point, he was concerned about what she was going to do to their father.

He made me promise that I wouldn't let her play with him.

I had no idea what the hell he meant by that but promised just the same.

When we arrived, it was too late. Hadley had her father tied up down in the basement.

Gerrick was here waiting for us when we arrived, and the solemn look on his face told me everything I needed to know. Whatever he was trying to protect her from had failed. He wouldn't elaborate, only telling me that it was Hadley's story to tell.

How many times am I going to be told the same shit?

It's obviously bad, and I can only imagine their father is dying a slow painful death.

A click echoes loudly in this otherwise silent building, bringing me out of my daydream. I look toward the noise, and suddenly the door opens.

All I see is red.

Blood.

Hadley slowly exits the room, her beautiful face void of emotion and completely covered in blood. I can't believe the sight before me. Her clothes are fucking soaked.

What the hell did she do to him?

The wild look in her eyes worries me.

Her pupils are dilated and wide like saucers, and I'm fixated on them. She reminds me of a wild animal, celebrating its kill. She's so fucking far out of it right now, you would swear she's high.

Not knowing whether it's safe to approach her, I stand, watching.

Hadley's chest heaves in and out with every deep breath she takes. Her hands are trembling by her side as the knife she's holding in one hand and the gun she has in her other slip from her grip.

I whisper her name from my lips, "Hadley."

She blinks, her irises shrinking back to normal and her vision now focusing on me.

"Sean," she breathes.

"I'm here, baby girl."

She hesitantly approaches me, the realization of what she has done dawning on her, and I watch as her demeanor quickly changes.

Each step Hadley takes is shaky, her body trembling as she looks between her blood-soaked hands and me. It's like she is in a trance as she watches her father's blood dripping through the cracks of her fingers onto the ground beneath. Large sobs escape her mouth when she finally reaches me, her body shaking in shock.

"What have I done, Sean?" her small voice trembles.

Pulling her in, hugging her tightly against me, I comfort her. "Only what needed to be done, beautiful girl."

Returning my embrace, she grips onto me tightly, suffocating me. Her sobs become tears.

Hadley's grief over what she has just done to her father racks her body, devastating her.

"From the state of you, I'm guessing your father is dead," my voice whispers into her hair.

I need to know what has happened, but I don't want to release her. I'm scared that if I break our contact, she will crumble.

I can't even imagine the torment she is subjecting herself to.

There's nothing I can do that will take away the pain of everything he has done to her over the years, or the pain she has inflicted on him today.

"I showed him how much of a monster I am," her shaky voice trembles.

Glancing up, she looks me dead in the eye. "I showed him what kind of a monster he had made me into."

I'm speechless.

I don't think I could move even if I wanted to.

Holding my gaze, Hadley stares straight through me. I may be physically holding my girl in my arms, but her mind is somewhere else.

I'm looking into a shell.

This is not the girl I love.

Pressing her face into my chest, Hadley and I stand at the bottom of the stairs just outside the basement. Her tears soak through my shirt, yet I hold on to her for dear life. Tightly, I draw her into me for comfort, attempting to make her feel safe. I'll continue to do this until she moves, or for as long as it takes for her to come back to me.

"Please don't go into that room, Sean," Hads finally whispers into my chest.

She's still trembling, but nowhere near as bad as she was when she first walked out of that room.

"I won't, Hads, but we need to leave. I need to get you cleaned up."

Those beautiful eyes that I fell in love with look up at me with such sadness in them. She's struggling, and I don't know if it's because she is finally free or because of what she has done.

Leading her up the stairs, we pass by my father and Hawke, who have been patiently waiting at the top of the stairs. Nodding, my father acknowledges the extent of what they will be walking into and moves past us to initiate the cleanup. I will no doubt see what damage Hadley did to her father later, but right now, the only place I need to be is beside the girl gripping onto me like her life depends on it.

Maybe it does.

Sitting on the edge of the porcelain bath in our hotel room, I gently caress Hadley's hair. With her eyes closed, she looks angelic, so I cautiously use the washcloth to wash away the last of the blood from her face.

I thought of getting in with her, just to comfort, but I didn't want to spook her. She's been quiet since we left the apartment where she slaughtered her father. To save her from prying eyes, my father arranged for Hadley to be escorted in via the back door of the hotel. Thankfully we managed to get into our suite before anyone saw us.

I honestly thought it would be more of a mission to get Hadley cleaned up, but I managed to coax her into the shower fully dressed with ease. Carefully I peeled off her clothing as she stood under the heated water, watching as the blood rushed off her down the drain.

When she looked into my eyes as as I guided her toward the bathtub, there was nothing but emptiness in her stare. I thought that maybe my touch would ignite something in her, but so far, nothing.

Watching her while she relaxes in the bubbles, I feel so much love and sadness for this girl. Her life has been filled with more drama and tragedy than I will ever experience, and I know she will need time to open up to me.

When the time comes, I'll be here waiting.

Nothing that she has done, nor what has been done to her, will ever come between us. When my life was a void, this girl brought life to me. When I believed I had nothing to live for, especially after Sherlyn died, she gave me a reason.

This girl lying beside me in this bathtub has given me everything I have ever dreamed of, and so much more. She fixed me even though I didn't believe I could be, and now I need to do the same for her.

Hadley is my ever after—well, for as long as she will have me, anyway.

I may be young, but I have faith in happily ever afters. I only have to look at my parents to know it's possible.

Just recently, my father told me the story of how he met the woman he swore to love and protect for the rest of his life. I don't recall how that conversation started, but I was more than happy to listen. My father and I have never bonded like this in the past, and it warmed my heart being able to have him confide in me the way he did.

He was telling me that Hawke, of all people, had dragged him to a concert, something my father was never a fan of.

That's where he saw my mother for the first time.

It took me some time to get my head around the fact that Hawke did anything that you would consider fun. According to my dad, Hawke has not always been this closed off. There was a time when that man led a different life, and yet again, I was told that it was someone else's story to tell.

This time, it was Hawke's.

At this particular concert, my mother was only nineteen and was sitting off to the side, watching as her brothers performed. It was back in the sixties when my uncles first made it big. They were only teenagers themselves, and my mother apparently was at every performance.

Dad was telling me he couldn't tear his eyes away from her, yet he struggled to get close enough to talk to her. He recalls nothing of the actual concert, only her. He himself was only nineteen as well at the time.

As the story goes, it took him another year before he found my mother again. He and Hawke were on spring break from college. They found themselves in Laguna Beach with some other friends, and that's when my father stumbled across her reading at one of the beachside cafes.

Taking the initiative, he struck up a conversation with her that lasted hours. Eventually, they moved on from the cafe but never left each other's side.

Forty-odd years later, they are still together and still very much in love. If that's not hope that I can have the same, then I don't know what is.

"Thank you, Sean," Hadley whispers, breaking through my thoughts.

Finally, she is speaking.

"You're welcome, beautiful, but what for?" my curious voice inquires.

"Saving me," she replies, turning in the water to lay her head on the side of the tub so she can look up at me.

"I will always come to you, Hadley. I will always protect you."

Instinctively, my hand caresses her cheek, swiping at the tears that are now streaming down her face.

"I love you with everything that is inside of me. Know that now before I tell you my story," she confides, drawing a deep breath before sitting up.

Helping her out of the tub, I pass her the towel, repeating the very same words in return. She says nothing as she guides me toward our bed. Dropping the towel, she climbs under the covers, naked, and encourages me to sit near her on the bed.

When I'm finally seated, I grasp her hand into mine and wait for her to start.

HADLEY

Holding my hand to comfort me, Sean sits patiently, waiting for me to talk. I feel ashamed for what I'm about to open up to him about, so I fix my vision firmly on the comforter instead.

"My story starts when I am sixteen years old," I begin. "And I was used as a payoff to cover a debt my father owed to his Colombian counterparts.

Expecting something, any kind of reaction, I look up to see nothing but love reflecting in my boy's eyes. Continuing, I tell him how my padre asked me to negotiate a deal with the Colombians on his behalf. He'd apparently had another meeting he couldn't get out of and needed me to step up and learn the family business.

I was excited to be given the opportunity and keen to prove that I could do it.

When I arrived at the hotel they were staying in, I found two men snorting coke through a straw. I'd never seen anything like it before, having been sheltered from that side of my padre's business.

They welcomed me into the room and asked if I wanted to join them.

I refused.

I never understood the need to inhale or inject substances into my body for the purpose of having a good time.

I never needed anything, drugs or alcohol, to have fun, but it was obvious these two did, and I thought at the time, who am I to judge. Sitting down across from them, I watched as they did two more lines each. It when then I started to speak about the deal my padre wanted me to negotiate.

When they laughed at me, I was shocked. I had no idea what they found so funny. It wasn't until they got up from where they were seated to sit beside me that I started to feel fear.

Only then did it dawn on me that I had been deceived by my padre.

They sat closer than I would have liked, and I could feel their hands touching me, running over my body. My fear rose when the one named Maitas chuckled and told me that I was payment for a debt my padre needed to settle, that I was there to show them a good time.

My padre had promised them that they could do whatever they wanted to me.

Everything in me that night wanted to fight them, but they were too strong and had me pinned between them.

Their hands kept touching me in places I didn't want them to, and every time I cried, it only encouraged them to do it again and again. Nothing I said or did stopped them, and instead of screaming out loud for help, I choose to do it in my head.

That was when I shut down and my body became limp.

The two men my father had prostituted me out to took my lack of retaliation as an invitation to start invading my body in ways I'd never thought possible. My screaming and crying became internal, and through the worst of it, a voice answered me.

At first, I thought I was hearing things, and then she spoke to me again—a calm, soothing voice who told me to concentrate on her voice and nothing else. She promised to take away my pain, but I had to let her take over. She assured me that I could rest, and she would take care of the two men violating my body.

I was so tired and in so much pain that I just said yes.

After that, everything was a bit of a blur until I awoke the next morning.

Regardless of what my padre told me, it took months for me to recall exactly what happened.

Stopping briefly, I grab the glass of water Sean is offering me. Waiting until I am finished with my water, he brings both my hands in his and squeezes.

It's not much, but it's enough, and it's his way of telling me he's still with me, so I keep going.

Although my body healed over time, mentally I had changed.

Gone was the sweet girl, and in her place was a hardened bitch.

Once I had full recollection of that night and what I did to those men, I found something inside of me I never knew I had.

Gerrick calls it an evilness, a darkness so terrible he feared one day I would become lost to it.

Over the years, I discovered how to rein my new dark side in, when to let her out and when to hold her back. I regret not allowing her to take care of Luca, but when I think about it, he never pushed me to that point of no return.

I became good at what I did, and it benefited me for a long time.

When we had my padre trapped in that room, I resisted the voice for as long as I could, but she was persistent, and in the end, I had to set her free.

I remember everything up until Gerrick leaving the room.

After that, it's fuzzy.

It's like I blacked out.

It's as if I was being shielded from having to live with what we had been done. Let's face it, regardless of whether it's me or another personality of me, it's still my body doing those things, making me fully responsible for my actions.

Will she come back?

Of that, I can't be sure.

For now, though, she's gone, my Nereza, and the last thing I remember her saying to me was "*You're safe now, sweetness.*"

When I finish, we sit in silence.

Anxiousness starts its upward swirl throughout my stomach as my head considers whether the boy who owns my heart and soul is going to walk out that door. He knows now what lives inside of me and what I have done. The relief I feel opening up to him like that is amazing.

I haven't felt this free—*ever*.

Just when I feel my chest constricting in pain from not knowing what is going on in Sean's head, he finally finds his voice.

"My mother once said, Hadley, that life is what we make of it. We carry our scars over our hearts to remind us of what we have survived. They are not there to trouble us but to show us that we have the courage and strength to fight. Our future starts from now. Everything before it has no impact on what we, together, can do."

His words bring tears to my eyes and a smile to my face.

Happiness floods my heart.

"Let's wipe our slate clean right now, Hads. Together, we move forward, not backward. I love you, and that's all that matters."

Lying beside me, my boy pulls me close, molding my body to his. Pulling the covers over us both, he tells me to rest, that we will be leaving early in the morning to head home.

"I love you too, Sean Valentine," I tell him as my eyes succumb to the heaviness pulling me under into sleep.

EPILOGUE

SIX MONTHS LATER

"Hadley, are you okay?" a worried female voice asks from behind me.

That voice belongs to Sophie, Sean's sister.

We are at their home in Solana Beach, and I have been staring out at the ocean for the better part of an hour.

It's beautiful here and more relaxing than I'd ever imagined.

"Yes, Sophie, thank you. I'm fine, just admiring the view before the ceremony," I reassure her.

Oh, did I forget to mention?

I'm getting married today!

I'm so excited to be marrying Sean, and in an hour, I will be a Valentine. Nothing could make me happier—well, maybe that and the precious bundle of joy I am carrying.

Yep, you heard me correctly.

After I told Sean about my past, we made love, and not the hurried, hard sex that I had become accustomed to. This was slow and all-consuming and exactly what I needed to start the healing process. It also seems that night we forgot how to use protection, and now I'm six months pregnant.

I couldn't be happier.

"You looked like you were somewhere else for a moment there, girl. You had me worried," she replies.

Not everyone was happy about our news to begin with, but Sean's madre put everyone in their place, telling them that this baby is a godsend and that we should all be basking in the beauty of it.

I tell you, some of the things that come out of that woman's mouth make me giggle, yet I love her more than I ever did my own madre. It's remarkable, but in the short time I've been with Sean, she has adopted me as one of her own.

Sophie here was hesitant at first, and for that I can't blame her, until she saw Sean and me together. She has been calling me her sorella ever since.

"I was, Soph, but in a good place. This is a life I never imagined I would have, and I'm pinching myself to make sure it's real."

"Oh, it's real all right, and by the way, you're stuck with that brother of mine. How you deal with his OCD issues I have no idea, but I wish you love and luck for the future." Sophie giggles.

I love how open Sophie is.

She's crass but loveable and has a hot-ass boyfriend to keep her on her toes. Man, that boy of hers is fine. There are times, though, when I feel responsible for the sadness I see on their faces when they remember their friend Sherlyn.

Her death has caused a hole that will take time to heal, especially in Stephen.

I was hesitant around him at first, until he pulled me aside and told me that he didn't blame me for his girl's death.

When he hugged me, I cried, which in turn made him cry.

Those tears were refreshing, he told me, because it meant he was healing. He told me that he would never forget Sherlyn, and her memory is what fuels him to move forward.

Laughing in return, I tell Sophie that I would be more than happy to take her fratello off her hands, even with all his quirks. Grabbing my hand, she leads me back inside to get ready. We are having the ceremony on this very balcony in front of everyone Sean, and now I call family.

I even managed to get Gerrick to fly up for it.

He looks gorgeous as he moves toward me.

"Hadley, you get fatter every time I see you. Surely that nephew of mine is ready to drop by now?" Gerrick shouts out.

Typical!

He's such an ass!

Laughing even louder, Sophie tells him good luck and excuses herself. She is going ahead and will meet me in her room.

All the boys were forced out to the guest house. The groaning we had to deal with over that made even Anthony, Sean's padre, laugh—until he was told to leave as well.

"You are such a dick, Gerrick," I curse him.

"You never tell a pregnant woman they are fat, not unless you have a *death* wish. Do you know nothing about pregnancy? I still have three months left, and for the last time, we don't know what we are having."

Smirking, he pulls me in for a hug and whispers, "I know, darling sorella of mine, I just like winding you up."

Punching him, I tell him to join the boys and I will see him soon. Kissing my cheek, he heads down the gorgeous staircase, slamming the front door on his way out. The noise brings both Sophie and Sarah out of the room, so I reassure them it's nothing and let them drag me back in to get me ready.

As we reach the door of Sophie's room, a voice whispers to me, *"Take care, Hadley. You're safe now,"* and I smile.

SEAN

The last thing I expected was to be standing here in front of the agency chaplain getting ready to exchange wedding vows.

I'm pumped—actually I'm freaked, but mostly I'm excited because today I'm marrying the love of my life and the mother of my unborn child.

I don't know which one of us was freaked the most when we discovered the pregnancy. We talked about different options, but in the end, decided to speak with my parents. My father was pissed at first, ranting about being irresponsible and not taking precautions. I think he was more disturbed at the fact that he had to think about another of his children having sex.

My mother, on the other hand, was beyond excited and saw it as a sign, a sign of good. She reassured us that no matter what choice we made, she and my father would be there to support us.

The fact that we were so young never entered her mind. That shouldn't surprise me, as she had Sophie at a young age.

The last six months have gone by quickly, and so much has happened.

After Hadley's father was removed from the family, Gerrick stepped up and took his place.

There was some rumbling among the family, but he proved that he was the right person for the job weeks later and has held a strong position ever since. I don't have to like what he does, but I no longer judge him for it. It would be hypocritical of me, seeing as I am marrying his sister.

Us getting married, well, that was my girl's idea.

We had come to Solana Beach two weeks ago to visit Sophie and the boys before Hadley couldn't travel. She loves the house and the beach, so I had Hawke fly us to the main land, and we've been here ever since.

During our first week here, we were walking along the beach at sunset when Hadley dropped to one knee and asked me to marry her.

Initially, I thought she was in pain, so I dropped down in front of her to make sure she was okay. I didn't hear what she said, only catching on when she held out the ring and repeated the words.

I was speechless, but found my voice quickly to say yes.

When I turn as the music starts, a hand clasps my shoulder in support, and I catch Stephen grinning at me. He and Hadley clicked straightaway, and deep down, I think she has been good for him.

My girl told me they spoke about Sherlyn, and I won't deny I was worried to begin with, but when you see these two together, it removes all doubt. When he is joking with Hadley, you see glimpses of the Stephen from before, and it gives me hope that he's going to be okay.

It was a no-brainer that he needed to be my best man, and he accepted straightaway. The fact that he did blew me away.

My sister makes her way toward us, a smile radiating on her face. She looks beautiful, and if the reaction from Ben, who is beside Stephen, is anything to go by, he agrees.

Man, those two have it bad!

Emerging at the top of the staircase is my stunning wife-to-be. How she managed to get up all those stairs without tiring herself out is beyond me, but she has, and now she is making her way toward me as well.

Standing beside her, with his arm linked with hers, is Gerrick.

He was the only one Hadley has told about the pregnancy and the wedding. In her eyes, she has no other family except him, and now mine.

Stopping beside me, the chaplain does his thing and asks who will give this woman to this man. Gerrick steps forward at that and tells him he does, making my precious one smile.

Under her veil, I can see a lone tear slide down her cheek as she kisses her brother and thanks him. He touches her cheek through the veil briefly and whispers, "You're welcome," before stepping back and taking his place with my parents.

All I can think of as the chaplain says the words that will bind us together forever is how lucky I am.

When he says the words, "I now pronounce you husband and wife," and tells me I can kiss my bride, I lift Hadley's veil.

Pulling her to me, I kiss the life out of her.

There are cheers and whistles around us as we pull away from each other. Holding my wife's gaze, I mouth the words *thank you* and lead her toward her new family.

The End